AN ISLAND HELLHOLE!

Captain Gringo slid the fresh belt Gaston handed him into his hot Maxim and, with a clear field now, proceeded to chop the hell out of the burning plantation house.

Don Diego's clothes were on fire as he ran out screaming, followed by two of his men who were also dressed in burning rags. The two men were armed, so Captain Gringo dropped them with one explosive burst. Don Diego ran on a few yards, fell face down among his opium poppies, and rolled over and over, crying out in agony.

Captain Gringo didn't shoot him. He didn't owe the fat, cruel Don Diego any favors.

Novels by
Ramsay Thorne

Published by
WARNER BOOKS

Renegade #25

HIGH SEA SHOWDOWN

Ramsay Thorne

WARNER BOOKS

A Warner Communications Company

WARNER BOOKS EDITION

Warner Books, Inc.
666 Fifth Avenue
New York, N.Y. 10103

 A Warner Communications Company

Printed in the United States of America

First Warner Books Printing: July, 1984

10 9 8 7 6 5 4 3 2 1

It was the Day of the Dead. So all day the narrow steets of San José had been crowded with noisy Costa Ricans living it up. Tin horns were still honking, strings of firecrackers were still going off, and señoritas were still screaming as mysterious strangers in skeleton masks felt them up.

The rather grotesque religious holiday was supposed to last all day and it would, even though by late afternoon the festivities were becoming a bit forced and the wiser heads in the crowd were starting to drop out. Little kids who'd been eating candy skulls and swilling soda pop all day were beginning to puke on people's rented costumes. Bigger kids who'd been swilling stronger stuff were threatening to become fighting drunks, and, naturally, as the shadows lengthened, the resident robbers and pickpockets would be crawling out of the woodwork.

And so, in his furnished room on the second floor of

La Posada Dulce, Captain Gringo was celebrating the Day of the Dead more sedately with his landlady and current paramour, a pleasingly plump brunette named Lucita. He'd have enjoyed Lucita's ample charms more had they been able to shut the grilled window above the big brass bedstead. But when two consenting adults find themselves in bed together on a tropic afternoon they need all the ventilation they can get, even if it stinks.

The faint sultry breeze blowing across the big blond Yank's bounding buttocks as Lucita moaned in ecstasy reeked of spent fireworks, puked sugar candy and rum, red pepper, and frying grease. None of which went with Lucita's rather cloying violet perfume and more earthy body odors. But a man had to do what a man had to do. So maybe if he slid another pillow under her Junoesque bare rump . . .

"Por favor, Querido," Lucita said, sighing as he reentered her from a more inspiring angle, "what you are doing to me feels most delicioso. But this is not what I came up here for and, en verdad, you have placed me in a most awkward position, Deek."

He smiled down fondly at her and asked, "Don't you like it with two pillows under you, my little propietaria?"

She sighed and spread her soft thighs wider as she dug her nails into his buttocks and replied, "You know all too well how much I like *this* position, you muchacho malvado! I was speaking of the position you have placed me in with the owners of this posada. As I was trying to tell you when you started tearing my clothes off just now, I do not own this place. I only manage it for most-greedy people who do not understand my warm feelings for you."

He said, "Speaking of warm feelings, it's just too

damned hot in here for this old-fashioned stuff. Let's try it dog style.''

Lucita didn't argue about that. But as he rolled her over on her hands and knees she insisted, ''I have to tell them *something*, Deek! You know if it was up to me alone, you and your little French friend could stay here forever without paying rent. But unless I can give the owners some idea when you and Gaston can pay . . . Oh, that feels so glorioso, Querido!''

That had been the general idea. He had to stall their landlady at least until his sidekick, Gaston, got back with news of a job or, at worst, another place they could hole up, free, until they got one. As he stood with his bare feet on the rug and his organ grinder in Lucita's big bare rump, thrusting with more skill than enthusiasm, Captain Gringo tried to figure out where the money from that last soldier-of-fortune job had gone. He and Gaston had been living pretty discreetly since making it back to the only country in Central America where they weren't wanted for everything but the common cold. But the one worm in the apple of Costa Rica was the simple fact that a working democracy with a free and easy popular government just didn't offer steady employment, or any employment at all, for professional fighting men. And despite its being an inexpensive place to rest up between jobs, a knock-around gent was expected to pay *something* for his bed and board even when he got to lay his landlady.

Great minds appeared to be running in the same channels that afternoon. Even as Lucita arched her back to take it deeper she said, ''I have to tell the owners something when I see them later this evening after the fiesta. When can I assure them they can expect at least part of the money you owe them?''

"Don't talk dirty while you're fucking," he growled, pounding her harder to change the subject to more pleasant matters. It only kept her quiet until she'd climaxed and fell forward across the crumpled sheets, sobbing how much she loved him. But the trouble with women was that they could be so ungrateful, as soon as they calmed down a bit. He'd just snuggled down beside her and lit a smoke when she said, "Oh, I've been meaning to speak to you about those expensive cigars you keep charging at the cantina downstairs, Deek. Honestly, don't you and that little Frenchman ever pay for *anything*?"

He put his free hand in her fuzzy lap to gain such advantage as he could before he sighed and said, "All right. I don't need a brick wall to fall on me. I can take a hint. As soon as Gaston gets back we'll be checking out."

It worked, for a moment. Lucita put her own hand on the back of his to encourage his soothing motions as she spread her thighs wider and said, "Don't be so sombrío. I never said I wished for to throw you out, Querido. I only said I had to promise the owners *something* this evening. Suppose I tell them you promised to pay by this time next week? Surely the check Gaston assured me was in the mail will have arrived by then, no?"

He sighed and said, "Gaston shouldn't have told you that, Lucita. We're a couple of bums. But I pride myself on being an *honest* bum. There isn't any check in any mail. I hope nobody who's at all interested in us has this address."

She began to fondle him, too, as she snuggled closer and said, "In that case I shall just have to lie *for* you, I fear. It is not easy for to get such a good job in San José, and they are sure to fire me in any case, once they discover I let you check in without any luggage *or* money!''

He snubbed out the smoke and kissed her before he said flatly, ''You're not going to get fired, Lucita. That's a promise. So what say we drop this tedious business talk and get down to business again with that sweet little tamale you're twitching at me?''

Lucita giggled and said he was just awful as he remounted her and hooked his elbows under her knees to put it to her deep, the way he knew she liked it. But even as she responded to him passionately, the saner corners of her mind were still stewing about what on earth she'd ever tell the owners. He kissed her hard to shut her up. And to shut himself up, too. It was hard to keep from reassuring a worried friend at such a time. But he couldn't tell her, until Gaston agreed, how they'd been holding out on her.

They did have a little money left. The trouble was, they didn't have enough to pay their bills and still have enough left over to get anywhere else. But he'd meant what he said when he'd promised Lucita her job was safe. So if Gaston came back from that meeting to say the deal was off and they weren't getting any front money after all, he'd just have to rob a bank or something, right?

Captain Gringo had meant it seriously when he told Lucita he hoped nobody at all interested in him had his current address. But even as the renegade soldier of fortune was enjoying his landlady's ample charms, a U.S. secret-service agent named Rumford was pinpointing the posada for his superior, Agent Purvis, on a wall map at the U.S. consulate across town.

Rumford said, "The renegade's there now. That little Frenchman he runs with left the posada a good three hours ago and our tails lost him in the fiesta crowd. I've got a team staked out around their hideout. We're ready to move in anytime you say, Chief."

Purvis looked pained and said, "Let's not be hasty, Son. We're Secret Service, not Justice or War. So leave us not be jumping any guns until we find out just what old Richard Walker, alias Captain Gringo, is up to here in San José."

Rumford, newer to the bananalands than his older and wearier-looking boss, frowned and said, "He can't be up to anything here in Costa Rica, Sir. He hides out here between jobs for the same reasons the intelligence community uses Costa Rica as a safe place to keep the files. Nothing too dramatic ever happens here."

Purvis turned from the wall map, went back to his desk, sat down, and opened a tobacco humidor on the green blotter as he chuckled dryly and said, "Yeah, the Spanish Empire sure screwed up Costa Rica when they were still running things. Sit down and have a smoke."

Rumford did as he was told and waited until he'd lit both their Havanas politely before he observed, "I'd hardly say the Spanish left this particular ex-colony in a mess, Sir. It's the only real working democracy down here. Except for the lingo and hot peppers, Costa Rica reminds me of Switzerland in some ways."

Purvis nodded and said, "You're learning, Son. Like I said, they screwed up. Spain's colonial policy was divide and conquer. So even after Latin America got rid of Spanish rule, most of 'em were left in one hell of a mess. It's the class and racial hatreds fostered by the old Spanish rule that make life so dramatic down here. But I guess they just weren't paying attention when they got around to settling Costa Rica. The name itself was a Spanish sarcasm. There were no riches here at all when they found the place. No gold or silver. Not enough Indians to bother saving and enslaving. In the end they used it as a dumping ground for cheated Spanish veterans. Giving a retired soldier or sailor a homestead in unmapped and unwanted jungle sure beat giving him a *pension* for life back in Spain."

Rumford looked puzzled as he said, "The Costa Ricans I've met so far don't seem very militant to me, Sir."

Purvis smiled fondly and said, "Yeah, they're pretty nice guys for the most part, and the girls are the prettiest in Central America. You know why? Good breeding, that's why. The people *running* the old and current Spanish Empire were and are a bunch of inbred jerk-offs. But the average enlisted vet with an honorable discharge tends to be a decent guy no matter who he works for. So as Spanish vets brought their white Spanish peasant wives over here to settle on their modest land grants, Costa Rica wound up decent too. Nobody wound up all that rich or all that poor. There weren't enough Indians to produce a sullen class of mestizo peones. The original settlers didn't have enough money or enough land to import slaves. They just buckled down, got to work, and wound up with a mighty nice little country here. They say Switzerland was an accident too."

Rumford repressed an impatient grimace as he said, "I'm sure that's all very interesting, Sir. But may I ask what it has to do with that renegade, Walker?"

Purvis shrugged and said, "For one thing, Costa Rica doesn't have an extradition treaty with the States.

Walker and that little legion deserter, Gaston Verrier, know it. So they've been very careful about busting any local laws."

Rumford said, "We wouldn't need help from the local police, Sir. He's alone at the posada right now and we have him boxed, so..."

"I hope you left orders nobody's to move in without my approval?" Purvis cut in with a worried frown. When Rumford nodded, he relaxed a bit but still looked annoyed as he said, "I keep telling people around here, but nobody listens. This is the U.S. Secret Service, Rumford. You don't keep secrets by holding public shootouts in the streets of a friendly power without letting their authorities in on it. You don't keep secrets by telling said authorities of said friendly power that you're a secret-service agent. Am I talking too fast for you, Son?"

"Nosir. I understand secret service reports only to Washington. But we have to do *something* about that goddamn Captain Gringo!"

"Why?" Purvis asked calmly.

Rumford blinked in surprise and gasped. "Why, Sir? The son of a bitch is a U.S. Army deserter wanted for murder, grand larceny, and God knows what all by now! Aside from the U.S. government, Mexico and half a dozen other greaser governments have reward posters out on him and that murderous little frog he runs around with!"

Purvis shrugged and said, "Some say Walker was framed on a bum rap. But that's neither here nor there. Like I said, our job is to gather intelligence, not bad guys, and those two soldiers of fortune aren't the only bad guys in this neck of the woods. I asked you to see if you could get a line on one Sir Basil Hakim, British subject, possible German agent, and all-around prick. So where is *he* right now?''

Rumford looked uncomfortable and said, ''We know his private yacht's moored down in Limón, Sir. If he's here in San José, he's holed up pretty good. We naturally checked all the better hotels in town, but . . .''

''Jesus,'' Purvis cut in with a groan, adding, ''I don't know how to tell you this, Son, but master criminals seldom check into hotels of any sort. Hakim's so fucking rich he doubtless owns one or more private houses in every town from here to Constantinople. Okay, so much for Hakim. How about that military attaché, Jager, at the German legation?''

Rumford brightened and said, ''Oh, he was easy to tail, Sir. Right now he's at the Spanish embassy. Been there all day, as a matter of fact. We spotted some British agents tailing him, too. So there must be something to that rumor about the young kaiser and His Most Catholic Majesty being up to something.''

Purvis drummed on his desk blotter thoughtfully as he stared at his telephone. Then he shook his head and told himself, aloud, ''No sense calling Greystoke of British intelligence. That wise-ass lies to us when the truth is in his favor. We've got *him* under surveillance, too. So, okay, we'll just sit tight and see who contacts those soldiers of fortune first.''

Rumford tried. He was learning how sneaky his older boss was. But he knew he'd never get any sleep that night unless he asked. So he asked what on earth anyone would want with scum like Captain Gringo and Gaston Verrier.

Purvis said, ''Something calling for the services of real professionals, of course. Something's up. Something big. Ever since that last hurricane, all sorts of strange bedfellows indeed have been running about like a mess of very sneaky alley cats with red ants under their tails. Our naval intelligence picked up some waterfront talk about some vessel, an important one, going down in that storm. Obviously the Brits, the spicks, and the square heads know more about it than *we* do. Hakim could be working for still another side, for all we know. He sure didn't come here to bid on coffee or bananas. Have you ever had the feeling you're the only kid on the block who doesn't know if that redhead on the corner puts out or not?"

Rumford grinned like a mean little kid and said, "I get it. Whatever may be up, it's safe to assume the Brits and Germans can't be in on it together. So one side or the other may want to hire Walker and the Frenchman to murder someone on the other, right?"

"Close enough, though they say Captain Gringo doesn't sign contracts like that. What they might want him for is unimportant. What's important is that we have him under surveillance. So when and if someone approaches our soldiers of fortune, we'll have *them* under surveillance, too! Get enough tails on enough people and we *have* to find out just what in the hell is going on."

He reached for the phone as he added, "We're going to need more field agents on this can of worms. I'd better have Limón and Puntarenas send us all the guys they can spare."

Rumford asked, "What happens to those two hired guns once we know who they're working for, Sir?"

Purvis asked the consulate switchboard operator to connect him through to the secret-service office in the coastal port of Limón and, as he waited, told Rumford, "It depends on who hires them to do what, of course."

"And once we know that, Sir?"

Purvis shrugged and said, "I told you why I didn't want them hit here in San José. Once they're out of Costa Rican jurisdiction, you can shoot 'em, stuff 'em, or eat 'em for supper for all I care."

"But what if they don't *leave* San José, Sir?"

"They will. Nobody ever hires Captain Gringo just to mind the store."

Secret-service agent Purvis was right. In yet another part of San José, two gray but very dangerous men regarded each other with mutual distaste as the sun went down outside. The sunset could not be seen from Sir Basil Hakim's inner sanctum. Oriental rugs and drapery worth a king's ransom covered every inch of the walls, floor, and ceiling. Perfumed candles provided dim illumination but failed to mask the scent of hashish and messy sex that haunted Sir Basil's office, harem, or whatever he chose to make of it. At the moment Sir Basil reclined on a mass of silk pillows, wearing bloodred silk pajamas stained here and there with dry semen. He was just too tall to qualify as a dwarf. His oversized head was about as satanic as one might expect, considering the gray Satanic beard and his record. Sir Basil Hakim was said to be either a Turk, a Russian, a Jew, or a Greek, depending on which group one's informant hated most. Born in Constantinople, or Alexandria, or wherever, Sir Basil was a British subject who'd been knighted for doing certain favors for people in London who were probably still paying blackmail to keep him quiet. One of the nicer things anyone had ever called Sir Basil was the Merchant of Death. In addition to his other vices, he sold arms to one and all in a truly democratic manner.

His unenthusiastic guest was Gaston Verrier, late of the French foreign legion, or any other army that would hire him. Although taller by far than his host, Gaston was one of those small gray men people fail to notice until too late. He'd killed his first man in the slums of Paris before he started shaving, and after a long hard life was cheerfully willing to concede that he was a very dirty old man. But he still thought he was a lot nicer than his host, and, in truth, few who knew Hakim would disagree. Gaston was fully dressed in tropic linens and was not sprawled across pillows like a lazy cat at the moment. He was seated on a hassock, albeit staring a bit like a cat, himself, as he waited for the shithead in the red pajamas to say something.

Hakim yawned and said, "It was so good of you to drop by, Old Bean. I have a little business proposition that might interest you and your friend, Dick."

Gaston grimaced and said, "I did not drop by. I was frog-marched here by two of your très grotesque hirelings, and I am so ashamed of myself I could spit. But merde alors, how was I to expect two six-year-olds in skeleton masks to pull guns on me in that adorable alley?"

Sir Basil chuckled and said, "They weren't children. They were midgets. I enjoy towering over my help, when I can, and you must admit my trap was rather ingenious, eh what?"

"Eh bien, I said I was too sentimental to shoot children on sight. But you and your adorable fellow dwarves kidnapped me to no purpose. I don't have any money at the moment, and not even my dear old mother would pay ransom for my somewhat battered body, if that is your new game.''

Hakim said, ''Dick's right about you, you know. You love to talk but you never *listen*. I said I had a deal to offer you lads. A thousand each, up front. A thousand a week until the job is done to my satisfaction. How do you like it so far?''

Gaston snorted in disgust and said, ''With anyone else, for a thousand dollars, I might drop my pants and bend over. But knowing *you*, it has to be something dirtier. Knowing my comrade, Dick, he will no doubt wash my mouth out with soap when he hears I have been talking to you!''

Sir Basil scratched his balls absently and said, ''At the moment the notorious Captain Gringo is surrounded by secret-service agents and under surveillance by both British and German intelligence. The Germans are working with the Spanish, of course, so we don't have to worry about *them*, eh what?''

Gaston didn't answer. So Hakim knew he had his undivided attention as he nodded and added, ''Naturally my own people are watching all those other people from surrounding rooftops, with scoped rifles. I don't think anyone's about to take our young friend without my full approval. But on the other hand, if we're not *friends* anymore . . .''

''What's the job, mon ami?'' Gaston asked flatly.

Hakim chuckled and clapped his hands twice. Two naked girls came through a slit in the drapes carrying a moving-picture projector between them. Neither was older than eleven or twelve, but their painted faces were world weary and their eyes were the eyes of old whores. One placed the projector on a pillow and angled it in position before crawling to the wall on her hands and knees to plug it in. Hakim noticed the bemused expression on Gaston's face as he stared at her immature but shapely rump and asked, "Would you like some of that, Gaston?"

Gaston looked away, scowling, to see the other naked child moving drapes away from an expanse of whitewashed bare wall. Gaston said, "Eh bien, are we to have our very own cinema this evening?"

Hakim nodded and said something to the girls in a language Gaston didn't know, and he knew lots of languages. As one of them blew out all but one candle, the other put a reel in place and flicked on the projection bulb before she began to crank the machine.

Gaston watched the improvised movie screen with interest as the flickering image of a very blond little girl sucking off a very black gentleman appeared. He grimaced and observed, "I knew it would be something dirty."

Hakim sighed and said, "Wrong reel," before cursing or ordering his young projectionist in that same odd tongue. The girl calmly changed reels, and this time the image was that of what looked like an old Monitor-class gunboat moving across the calm waters of some bay or inlet. Hakim said, "My people didn't take these. They bought them from a German naval officer who finds it difficult to keep a wife and two mistresses on a lieutenant commander's salary."

Gaston frowned and said, "The vessel would seem to be sinking, non?" But as the image on the wall kept dropping deeper in the water, Hakim said, "It's not sinking. It's a submarine. Young Kaiser Willy's stolen the American Holland boat design, improved it, and has his engineers designing around Edison's patented storage batteries. This particular tub was running on outright copies of Edison's patent. No doubt the Germans would have some explaining to do if the Yanks found out about it, eh what?''

Gaston waited until the submersible flickered all the way under, save for the periscope he'd assumed up until now to be a flagstaff. Then he shrugged and said, ''Everyone knows Der Kaiser likes new toys. Who built that très soggy gunboat for him, you?''

Sir Basil looked pained and replied, ''As a matter of fact, my Woodbine Arms, Limited, did bid for the contract. We were underbid by a German firm I'd never heard of. I'd most certainly like to find out how they did it. We bid as low as we could, assuming, of course, that once we had the contract we'd be able to work in the usual cost overruns. But those sons of bitches from Linke-Stettin promised to build submarines for the price of tugboats, and, worse yet, as you see, they seem to be *building* them!''

''Ah, but of course, once they began, a few unforeseen expenses cropped up, hein?''

''No, God damn it! Linke-Stettin brought the fucking submarines to completion on time and to specs! It's *impossible* to build a seagoing submarine that cheaply. But they did it, and I have to know how!''

Gaston shrugged and said, ''Do not look at *us,* then. We are soldiers of fortune, not naval architects. Dick is très good with a machine gun and I, in all modesty, can be formidable with artillery ordnance. It would appear you are more in the market for a pair of slide-rule types, non?''

''I have all the naval architects I need. I need you and the notorious Captain Gringo to get them within reach of that bloody underwater gunboat.''

''Merde alors, in *Germany*?''

Hakim laughed harshly and said, "Closer than that," before he indicated to the naked girls that the show was over. As they put away the gear and vanished back into the drapery again, Hakim told Gaston, "Everyone who subscribes to the Hearst newspapers knows the Yanks are spoiling for a war with Spain over Cuba. Everyone who knows the Spanish navy knows a determined Irish drunk could sink it with a hod of bricks. Der Kaiser didn't vote for Cleveland, and just signed a treaty with his chum, the king of Spain. In exchange for Spanish neutrality in any future war with France, the Germans have been beefing up the Spanish military forces with smokeless powder, armor plate from Krupp, and some submarines from Linke-Stettin. Need I say more?"

"Oui, even the troublemaking kaiser has to know a few unproven weapons can't help the tottering Spanish Empire at this late date. The U.S. isn't going to hit them with drunken Irishmen. They just built a très moderne navy of their own!"

Hakim shrugged and said, "True, but young Kaiser Willy would doubtless like to see how some untried ideas work before he uses them himself in the big war he seems to be planning. His motives are neither here nor there. The point is that the Germans delivered a sister ship to the one I just showed you on film. It was last seen by my own agents in the Spanish port of La Coruna. My engineers assured me no submarine built to the current state of the art can cross the Atlantic under its own limited power. But a few weeks ago, just after that hurricane, a Honduran patrol boat picked up a Spanish sailor adrift in a life raft near the Bahía archipelago. He was in bad shape when they found him and died a few days later. But not before he told them he'd been an engine wiper on a Spanish submarine driven on the rocks of the Bahías during the storm. The Hondurans had a look. They failed to spot any sign of a stranded anything. So it's on the bottom, in shallow water, somewhere off the Bahías. You know the Bahías, of course?''

Gaston made a wry face and replied, ''I try to avoid them at all costs when forced to pass near. None of them are too civilized, and the Black Caribs inhabiting some of the smaller Bahías are still très savage.''

Hakim reached under a silk cushion as he nodded and said, ''That's where you and Captain Gringo come in. I'm sending a clandestine team to locate and salvage or at least examine that Spanish vessel. If it is a submarine and not the ravings of a dying man, Woodbine Arms is in an awful mess. I know what they say about me, but I do build pretty good weaponry. I have to know how Linke-Stettin not only underbid me but built a better sub than anyone working for me can.''

He handed Gaston a perfumed envelope and added, ''There's two thousand U.S. worth of local currency in here. The arms and ammo you lads will need to act as security for my engineers will be aboard the Greek sponge schooner you'll all be using as a front. Go back to the posada, tell your friend about the deal and give him his half, then wait for further instructions. My people will give you your .38 and dagger back as you leave.''

Gaston took the money, of course, but said, ''Mais you just told me the adorable posada is surrounded by très fatigué secret agents avec guns, non?''

Hakim shrugged again and said, ''A mere detail. Let *me* worry about it. *You* just worry about convincing Captain Gringo his bread is buttered on my side, for now.''

Gaston sighed and said, "That may not be easy. Dick is not what one could call an admirer of yours, hein?"

Hakim said, "Tell him it's his patriotic duty. I know he was treated rather unjustly by the U.S. government. But surely he can't want the U.S. Navy steaming into a death trap in the near future. I still have a few bones to pick with you lads, too, you know. But for once we seem to be on the same side. *I* don't want Spanish submarines complicating the Cuba Libre movement, either."

Gaston grinned crookedly and replied, "Mais non, not unless Woodbine Arms gets to sell them to Spain, hein?"

Sir Basil Hakim scratched his crotch again and said calmly, "Well, business is business. But if I can convince Der Kaiser and His Most Catholic Majesty that I can build subs better, they'll probably scrap the ones Linke-Stettin built, and, well, I doubt if even I can replace enough subs to matter in time, if the Yanks will just shake a leg."

He yawned, clapped his hands again, and, as the two little naked girls came in to rejoin him on the pillows, added, "You'd better go now. I'm getting an erection. You have your orders. You know what will happen if you mess the mission up."

Back at the posada, Captain Gringo didn't like the idea at all. Lucita had left him alone and well sated by the time Gaston arrived to hand him a thousand and suggest he put on his pants. The tall Yank went along with Gaston at least that far. He even put the welcome funds in his money belt. But then he said, "Before you suggest it, I agree, this time, a double cross is our best bet. We don't owe Hakim anything but a hard time, and that story has to be a lie."

Gaston said, "True, but at the risk of sounding soft in the head, I suggest we go along with him at least until he gets us *out* of here!"

Captain Gringo finished dressing, blew out the lamp, and moved to the grilled window as he growled, "Shit, that story about this place being surrounded could be just a ploy to keep us here until he's ready to send for us."

"But what if it is not, my old and cynical?"

Captain Gringo peered out through the grille. A couple of drunks in skeleton masks were reeling down the otherwise deserted street. Another grille much like this one overlooked the same scene from across the way. Anyone staring out through it was of course as invisible to him as he hoped he was to them. He swept the roof line above it with more interest, muttering, "The trouble with Hakim is that he lies so cleverly. I don't see shit. But that still works two ways."

Then an evening star hanging just above the tiles across the way winked off and on again. Captain Gringo swore softly and added, "God damn it to hell, there *is* something pussyfooting around over there. Could be a cat, of course."

Gaston asked, "Do you really think we should bet our adorable asses on it being a pussycat instead of a pussyfoot, avec a gun?"

Captain Gringo shook his head and said, "We're better off staying forted up behind these thick walls for now. But I'm missing something here. If someone has us boxed, why haven't they moved in before this?"

"Perhaps they don't like noise? You have the reputation of being très rude to people who burst in on you uninvited, non?''

"Maybe. But just a little while ago you were gone and they could have literally caught me alone with my pants down. Did Hakim say who the hell those guys are?"

"Oui, spies, not lawmen. One gathers the reason they see no need to move in is that their orders are to follow us, not shoot us, hein?"

"Okay, so why don't we just cut out and *let* 'em follow us? How far can anyone tail a couple of guys through the dark streets of a town they know? Remember that cantina with the unlocked skylight over the men's room?"

Gaston nodded but said, "The secret agents are not the only problem, Dick. He ordered us to stay put until he sends for us, and *his* people won't try to follow us if they observe us crossing Hakim double with his *money* on us, hein?"

Captain Gringo sat on the rumpled bed and lit a smoke. Then he shrugged and said, "Well, we have a whole night ahead of us and nobody can shoot us in here without giving us at least an even chance at 'em. Tell me some more about this Bahía archipelago."

Gaston found a bentwood chair, lit his own claro, and said, "Oh, I agree we have to desert the mission before it reaches the Bahías! The species of perversion only gave us two lousy thousand, and I would not go there for *ten*! The Bahías are a chain of reefs and islands great and small off the northeast coast of Honduras. Honduras owns them, on the map, but does not really govern them, since governing the Bahías is not possible. The larger Bahías are inhabited by white or mestizo wreckers and occasional fishermen, descended from pirates or fugitives from justice. The smaller islands are inhabited by Black Caribs descended from runaway slaves and unreconstructed Carib Indians. You know, of course, what *Carib* means in Spanish?''

''Sure, 'cannibal.' But none of the Caribs I've met so far seemed to really want to eat me. I think they were just after my shoes.''

''Oui, they've picked up a bit of culture since Columbus met and named them. But they are still coastal pirates who make the adorable sea rovers of the Barbary Coast look like sissies. Black Caribs are, if anything, more savage. The original tribe was simply truculent and interested in loot, or perhaps fresh meat. The runaway slaves they mixed with were bigger, given to strange African religious notions and instilled with a blind hatred for their former masters, or anyone with the same complexions.''

Captain Gringo shrugged and said, ''They still have to be nicer guys than anyone who'd work for Hakim. He said we'd be working from a ship, right?''

''Oui, but what of it? If the vessel he wants salvaged is in water shallow enough to find, it has to be within reach of Carib sailing canoes from the Bahía shores, non? Hakim said he was sending a mere schooner. A schooner moored alone in Carib waters is just what they consider meat on the table. Unless you have some mad desire to try your shooting skills on très dark targets paddling silently in the dark, I suggest we cross Hakim double somewhere between here and the coast. I know a house of ill repute in Limón with a secret passage for the use of discreet married clients.''

Captain Gringo said, ''We'll cross that bridge when we come to it. We've got to get out of *here* alive first.''

Then he stiffened as they both heard a firm knock on the locked door.

Captain Gringo rose, drawing his .38 from its shoulder rig as he stood out of line with the thin wood panels and growled, "Quién es?"

A feminine voice on the far side replied in English, "Hakim sent us. Let us in."

Gaston had risen to cover the door with his double-action revolver. So Captain Gringo opened the door from the far side and two women dressed in fiesta costume came in fast, slamming the door after them. They both wore their skeleton masks pushed up on their scalps to expose their faces. In the dim light it was still tough to judge what they looked like. Captain Gringo asked, "Aren't you girls out a little late, even for the Day of the Dead?"

The one closer to him said, "A few natives are still wandering about dressed like this, hoping their luck will change. The chaps surrounding this place no doubt took us for a pair of whores checking in. This *is* a public inn, you know."

Captain Gringo nodded but said, "I get your disguises. But how often does one puta check into a posada with another, Miss, ah . . . ?"

"Call me Vera, and this is Sarah. We didn't just check in as two women together, of course. We came in with a couple of Hakim's trigger men. Take off your clothes. Both of you."

Captain Gringo laughed incredulously and asked, "Just like that? I don't even know if you're pretty, but even if you are, this is a mighty dumb time to play slap and tickle!"

Vera stamped her foot impatiently and threw a bundle he hadn't noticed before past him onto the bed as she insisted, "Hurry! The other two men are just down the hall in their underwear. Naturally one is tall and the other short. I'm sure their costumes will fit you both."

Captain Gringo caught on, laughed, and said. "Gotcha. Can we keep our own underpants on, if you have to watch?"

Vera told him to stop screwing around. So he moved to the bed, untied the loosely bound bundle, and held the clown costume up to examine. He laughed again and said, "This one's your size, Gaston. It looks like I get to be a full skeleton and, yeah, here's the two masks. Pretty slick."

The two soldiers of fortune started undressing as the two women fussed at them to hurry. When they got down to their shorts and guns, Sarah grabbed their linen suits and planter's hats to tear out of the room.

Captain Gringo said, "I don't see what's the hurry, Vera. If this works, this works. If it doesn't, what's the rush?"

Gaston added, "True. My mother always said that there was no sense in rushing to one's execution."

Vera said, "You lot won't be going anywhere for some time. We have to let your doubles lead everyone surrounding this place on a wild goose chase, and the German agents are rather thick. So they'll have to move out slowly."

Captain Gringo sat back down on the bed in just his boots, shorts, and shoulder rig as he said, "Right. The costumed guys who checked in here with a couple of pickups shouldn't leave in less than an hour or so, unless they want anyone watching to think they're undersexed."

Gaston had moved over to the window in his own underwear and gun rig. So he suddenly laughed and said, "Mon Dieu, when Hakim tells people to move they most certainly move fast! Come have a peek, Dick, this is très amuse!"

Captain Gringo joined Gaston at the grille, with Vera trailing behind, just in time to see one tall guy in linen and a planter's hat whip around the far corner with a short guy dressed the same. A few moments later a door across the way opened and three other guys dressed a bit more native popped out to stroll casually after the decoy Captain Gringo and Gaston.

Captain Gringo grinned and turned to ask Vera where their doubles were going. He could see her face now, and it wasn't bad, as she replied, "Railway station. They're to catch the night train to Puntarenas, on the west coast. Two more of our people will board the train with them to supply them with fresh costumes in the men's room. Then all four of them, complete strangers to the agents tailing you and Gaston, will simply enjoy a quiet trip to the west coast, catch a few winks, and ride back again."

Gaston said, "I like it. Where is your companion, the mysterious Sarah, M'mselle?"

Vera said, "In your room, next door. Covering the alley to the rear. Your own window overlooks it, you may recall."

Gaston said, "Oui, I think I shall join her, then. I too find the sight of Boche creeping down dark alleyways très amuse."

Suiting actions to his words, Gaston scooped up his costume, mask, gun, and money belt to leave Captain Gringo alone with Vera.

Vera asked, "Do you imagine he'll get fresh with poor Sarah, Captain Gringo?"

"Call me Dick. He might. How poorly Sarah feels

about it depends on how she feels about distinguished older men. Is it true all you girls who work for Hakim have to apply for the job in his bed?''

She sniffed and said, ''Don't be disgusting. Sir Basil pays well, but not *that* well. You may as well put your new pants on, too, by the way. I'm not paid to go to bed with anyone.''

He chuckled and moved over to the bed by himself. The he rummaged through the suit-pocket contents he'd dumped on the bed for a light and relit the oil lamp on the bed table as he sat back down. Vera asked what he expected to see as she stood near the foot of the bed, hands on hips. He looked her over and said, ''Not bad. I admire redheads no matter what color hair they have. But I really need some light on the subject because I have to write a note for my landlady.''

He found an envelope in the drawer of the bed table. He opened his money belt and counted out the rent he and Gaston owed and them some. He stuffed the cash into the envelope, picked up a pencil stub, and wrote on the envelope, explaining how something unexpected but profitable had just come up in El Salvador. Then he sealed the envelope, placed it by the lamp where Lucita would be sure to find it, and told Vera, ''I don't expect my landlady to go to the police about us checking out so suddenly. But if she does, my white lie will fit our heading for the west coast.''

The redhead shrugged and said, ''I suppose so. But why do you have to leave any money if your landlady isn't here?''

He smiled up at her crookedly and observed, ''I see you've been working for that creep, Hakim, for some time. Don't try to figure it out. Us human beings don't understand *your* kind, either.''

She sniffed and said, "Thank you. Hypocrites like you make me sick, too. What time can we expect your landlady to burst in here? Nobody told us the two of you got on so well, and we were naturally expecting her to return to her own quarters down by the front door."

He glanced sheepishly at the envelope by the bed lamp and said, "You're a pretty good detective, Vera. I don't know when she'll be back. She didn't say."

Vera frowned thoughtfully as she ran her wide-set hazel eyes over Captain Gringo's naked chest and shoulders. Then she said, "She'll no doubt get back as soon as she can manage. Put on your costume. We'd better get out of here a little sooner than planned. I don't like killing witnesses if it can be avoided."

That sounded reasonable. So Captain Gringo slid on the black sateen costume with white bones painted down the front and back, put on the papier-mâché skeleton mask, and said, "Boo."

Vera didn't laugh. She pulled her own mask down over her face and turned to open the door, looking like Death dressed up flamenco. Captain Gringo filled the handy side pockets of his costume and rose to follow her, casting a last wistful glance at the rumpled sheets he'd never get to rumple again.

They went next door and rapped on Gaston's door. They heard a girlish giggle and then Sarah said they'd be with them in a minute. Gaston didn't say anything. His mouth was probably too busy. Vera knocked again and snapped, "Right *now,* God damn it!" and the girl on the other side answered, "Spoilsport!" but came out a moment later with Gaston following her, buttoning up his clown costume. As they all went down the dark back stairs together, Sarah whispered to Vera, "It's true what they say about Frenchmen. How did *you* make out, Vera?''

Vera told her to shut up. As she was about to open the back door, Captain Gringo said, "Hold it. Bad move," and the redhead snapped, "We have to get *out* of here, dammit!"

He said, "Sure, but we'd better do it right. Someone could still have the place staked out. If they do, they'll be expecting those two whores and their customers to leave by the same door they came in, right?''

Vera told him to watch who he was calling a whore, but led the way along the downstairs corridor toward the front as Sarah whispered, "What do we say at the front desk?''

Gaston took her arm and answered, "Nothing, assuming you and those other gentlemen paid in advance for the temporary use of some bed linens. Who has the keys?''

Vera said she did. Captain Gringo took them from her and muttered, "Gaston's right. Put a little wiggle in your walk and I'll just drop the keys on the desk without stopping.''

It worked. Lucita's night clerk was reading a magazine and barely looked up as they passed, dropping the keys on his desk. With luck, he might not even tell Lucita about two guys and two putas checking in for a quick roll in the feathers upstairs.

Out on the dimly lit street it got more complicated. As the four of them moved down the posada steps, a hansom cab pulled to a halt in front of them and *Lucita*, of all people, got out!

She looked a little startled, too, to see four skeleton masks staring at her. But she must have been eager to get back upstairs. So she asked if they were waiting for a cab and, when Vera said they were, politely left the cab door open for them, wished them well, and almost ran for the door.

Vera gave the driver an address and the four of them piled in. As they drove away, Gaston laughed and said, "Eh bien, it's about time things went right for a change. I could not have planned it better with a stopwatch!"

"Utshay upshay," muttered Captain Gringo, pointing up at the open hatch in the roof of the hansom. So as the steel-rimmed wheels rattled on, Gaston and Sarah snuggled on the jump seats facing Vera and Captain Gringo, and proceeded to feel each other up some more. Vera sniffed and turned her gaze from them to ask Captain Gringo if that had been his landlady back there. When he nodded, she sniffed again and muttered, "I might have known. A woman can always tell when another's in heat. Wasn't she a little fat for you?"

He shrugged and said, " 'Pleasantly plump' might describe her more politely. What's it to you? Have you got something skinnier lined up for me?"

She swore under her breath and said, "Not bloody likely. I'll be only too happy once we get you to your new address and I'll have seen the last of you!"

She must have been even more pissed off than she let on. For it was little blond Sarah, of all people, who spotted a passing street sign over Gaston's shoulder as they passed it and murmured, "Coo, that's odd. We're supposed to be going the other way, aren't we?"

Vera glanced out on her side and said, "I'm not sure where we are at the moment. One stucco wall looks much the same as any other, and I confess I haven't been paying attention as we've swung a few corners.

One assumes that when one gives a cabdriver an address, that's where one is going, what?''

Captain Gringo murmured, ''Gaston, start telling us a dirty story, loud. Do I have to say why?''

Gaston replied, ''Mais non. Have any of you heard the one about the mother superior and the nearsighted young priest?''

Captain Gringo had, but he wasn't listening as Gaston made it sound as if four innocent lambs were going quietly to the slaughter, sharing dirty stories and sniggers. Sarah sniggered good. Vera watched, tense and silent, as the tall American drew the .38 from under his costume and pulled his mosquito-booted feet up on the leather seat between them. He waited until the driver swung yet another corner into a darker and narrower street. Then he shot up to his full height, with his head and shoulders out the open roof hatch, and said, ''Boo!'' as he shoved the .38 muzzle almost up the nose of the driver perched behind the flat-topped hansom.

The driver reined in, gasping, and said, ''Nombre de Dios, Señor! For why are you pointing a gun at me?''

''I'll ask the questions, Amigo. Who are you working for?''

''Working for, Señor? I work for nobody but myself, and my customers, of course. Is this a holdup, Señor?''

''Not yet. Who's laying for us at the end of the line, holdup men or someone who may have paid you *more* to deliver us? Take a deep breath and think before you answer. I shoot people who lie to me.''

The driver said, ''I know, you have been drinking all day and now you think someone's after you, eh? I swear on the grave of my sainted mother that I have no idea what you are talking about, Señor.''

So Captain Gringo shot him, grabbed the reins with

his free hand, and was out of the hatch and in the driver's seat before the driver's body made it to the cobbles with a dull thud.

Down in the cab, Vera shouted, "Have you gone crackers?" as Captain Gringo wheeled the cab around and whipped its horse to a run with the slack in the reins. Behind them, back the way the treacherous driver had been taking them, someone shouted. He knew it wasn't their driver. Nobody ever shouted once he'd been shot between the eyes.

The sounds of running steel-shod hooves and steel-rimmed wheels over cobbles popped doors and windows open with monotonous regularity as Captain Gringo raced for the darker parts of San José. He swung into a narrow street with no lights at all, slowed to a walk, and drove two more blocks before he reined in and called down, "Okay, everybody out!"

He climbed down himself and proceeded to tether the reins to an old pepper tree as Gaston helped the girls out, asking, "Was this trip really necessary, Dick?"

Captain Gringo said, "It was. You know this town better than I do, Gaston. So are we lost or not?"

Gaston looked around and said, "Merde alors, I, Gaston, am never lost. What was that address again, Vera?"

Vera gave it to him, adding that both of them were obviously mad, and Gaston said, "Eh bien. Follow me, my children. It is not too far to walk, and, from the way my adorable young speed demon just acted, one gathers we had better start walking, hein?"

Captain Gringo said that was for damned sure as he took Vera's elbow and fell in behind Gaston and Sarah. The redhead snapped, "I can see well enough, damm-it," but he said, "We're supposed to be a couple of gay caballeros walking our girls home from the fiesta. So shut up and look *happy,* dammit!''

She snuggled closer, but asked, "What was that all about back there? Do you think that driver was setting us up for a robbery or worse?''

He said, "Worse. I know you didn't think much of Lucita, but if the game had been robbery or rape, that driver never would have brought her back to her posada safe and sound. Somebody who knew she was my landlady tailed her to the home of her employers. Then they set it up so one of their confederates would be driving the first cab out front as she left. They weren't after Lucita. They were after Gaston and me. They probably gave the driver orders to deliver anyone who matched our description at all to whatever reception they had planned down that dark street on the wrong side of town. So don't ever call Sarah dumb again. She may be warmer-natured than some people I know, but she's got good eyes, and she saved our necks back there!''

Vera sighed and said, "I'm the one who was too stupid to look where we were going. But what could have gone wrong with Sir Basil's plan? Everyone was supposed to follow our confederates wearing your clothes!''

"Some of them may have," he soothed, adding, "Hakim told Gaston we had more than one bunch to deal with. Some knock-around guys are smarter than others or, hell, they may have just been covering all bets. Knowing we were holed up at the posada, they may have just decided not to let *anybody* get away, see?''

"They sound rather ruthless, don't you think?''

"It's a ruthless game. What do you call the guy *you*

31

work for, Santa Claus? I must say it's getting sort of interesting, though. If there wasn't something to that crazy story about a German-built Spanish sub, they wouldn't be playing so rough!''

Gaston led them around a corner, through an alley black as the pit, and back to another street with better lighting albeit cinder pavement. He said, "This calle runs in line with the much nicer one you adorable creatures seem to have rented quarters on. Let me see, there should be a slit between the walls along in here somewhere—a man who sometimes finds himself far from home with a mad desire to urinate has to keep such details in mind—and, voilà, I told you I am never lost!''

The rest of them had to take that on faith as Gaston led them through a crooked, dark, and seemingly endless passage between rough stucco walls that smelled of stale piss and worse. But when he finally led them out to a paved street again, Sarah marveled, "Oh, how clever! That's our place, over there on the far side to the left!''

Both girls started forward. But Captain Gringo stopped them and said, "Hold the thought. Is there a back entrance to that courtyard over there?''

They told him there wasn't. So he said he guessed they'd just have to chance it as he removed his mask and held it over his cocked .38.

But nothing happened as they cut across, entered the open gateway of the court, and waited until Vera unlocked a massive oak door and led them into pitch blackness. Captain Gringo stood well clear of her, gun in hand, as she struck a match and lit a hall lamp. Then he picked it up and said, "Stay here. I'm going to toss the premises before we sit down to toast marshmallows.''

Gaston and Sarah did. But Vera insisted on following him, fussing, as she insisted that each and every room he entered, armed and dangerous, was secure. When they got to the crapper, he said, "Well, when you're right you're right. But you sure are a trusting soul, considering the business you're in."

Vera's hazel eyes blazed as she spat back, "There you go with sarky remarks again! Sarah and I are troubleshooters for Woodbine Arms, not hired guns! *You're* the one who murdered that poor driver back there!"

He said, "Touché, but he wasn't a poor driver. He was a big fibber, and he had to go because you'd given him this address. Assuming you haven't given it to anyone *else* we have to worry about, what happens now?"

She said, "You're to stay here until other Woodbine people come for you in the morning. Hopefully early. They'll have tickets for you and Gaston on the morning train to Limón. It should be safe for you to move out by then."

"In this skeleton suit?"

She laughed despite herself and said, "Naturally they'll bring another change of costume. Shall we rejoin the others?"

He said, "May as well; I don't need to use this crapper at the moment." So they moved down the long narrow hall to where they'd left Gaston and Sarah. They weren't there. They'd moved into the small front parlor and were on the settee by the fireplace. They were not toasting marshmallows.

Captain Gringo said, "Cut that out, Gaston. This place checks out okay. It's laid out something like a New York railroad flat. Long hall to one side running

front to back with the rooms lined up along it. The crapper's at the end of the hall. Narrow ventilating slit above
the sink. Nobody fatter than a cat could get in or out that
way. No doors or windows save for the ones up front.
So we're forted pretty good, and Vera here says we
only have to stay one night.''

Gaston felt up the giggling Sarah some more as he
grinned and said, ''Très bien. In that case this little
cabbage and I shall take the nearest bedroom, hein?''

Vera shook her head and said, ''You'll do no such
thing. There are only two bedrooms. So the plan was
for you boys to take one while we girls spent the night
in the other, with the door locked!''

Sarah pouted and told Vera to speak for herself as
Gaston fixed her with a sardonic smile and said, ''Doesn't
that sound most perverse, M'mselle? Dick and I are
good friends, as you know, but every time I suggest we
go to bed together he beats me up!''

Sarah laughed and said, ''I'm no bloody lezzy, either. Come on, Gaston, I'll show you to the bedroom
with the softest bed.'' So the two of them rose from the
settee and scampered out, hand in hand, as Captain
Gringo laughed.

Vera didn't. She said, ''Damn, I might have known
Sarah would go into heat on me again. All right, you'll
just have to kip out here in the parlor. I'll fetch you
some blankets from the one bedroom left.''

He said, ''No you won't. That love seat can't be five
feet long and I'm well over six. A guy can't run for his
life worth a damn on cramped legs, Doll. So I'm taking
the bedroom. *You* can sleep anywhere you want.''

He moved out to the hall before she could answer.
He remembered the two bedroom doors from his earlier
exploration. So he twisted the first knob he came to,

opened the door, and said, "Oops. Sorry, Gaston," and closed it quickly. But not before Vera, behind him, got a good look at what Gaston and her chum, Sarah, were doing without bothering to undress first. She blanched and said, "Oh, how disgusting!"

Captain Gringo didn't answer. He opened the next door and stepped inside, unbuttoning his skeleton suit as he moved toward the big four-poster. He pulled the quilted comforter off the sheets and held it out to Vera, saying, "Here. I won't need this with no cross ventilation on a tropic night."

She took it but said, "You're just awful. Haven't you a shred of gallantry left?"

He said, "You were the one who said I was a nut for paying my bills. You're probably right that there's a little self-serving hypocrisy in the Robin Hood act. So I'm trying to reform."

She said, "You . . . bastard! That settee is hard and lumpy!"

"That's why you wanted *me* to sleep on it? Look on the bright side, Vera. At least you're shorter than me."

He sat on the mattress of the four-poster, bounced, and said, "Yum yum yum. If that other bed's softer it's too soft for me. Like Goldilocks said, this is just right."

He bent to pull off his mosquito boots. Then he peeled off the grotesque fiesta costume, wadded it up, and placed it on the bed table with the mask on top of it. As he stood in his shorts to unbuckle his money belt and gun rig, Vera stamped her foot and said, "Dammit, I want that bed!"

He shrugged and said, "I'll let you use *half*. It's big enough."

She blushed and said, "Not bloody likely! I don't want to be raped in my sleep!"

He frowned and said, "Don't be so egotistical. Did I say I owed you any favors?"

Again she laughed despite herself and said, "Pooh, you're not going to try to tell me you weren't sleeping with that dumpy Spanish girl back at that posada!"

He shrugged, slid his money belt and gun rig between the headboard and the mattress, and slid himself between the sheets as he said, "I didn't do anything to Lucita she didn't want me to do. We were good friends."

"I'll bet. Did you ever enjoy her the way Gaston was just treating poor Sarah?"

"You'd better ask Sarah in the morning if she spent the night in agony. I don't talk about what I may or may not have done to a lady who might have been a real pal."

Vera sneered and said, "It's small wonder you're ashamed to go into detail about your sordid relationship with that fat peasant girl! How could a white man sink so low?"

"Old Lucita wasn't so low, with a couple of pillows under her. She was white, sort of, and a lot nicer than you. Built better, too. So please shut the door as you leave. It's been a long hard Day of the Dead and I gotta catch forty winks before I'll feel alive again."

She called him a bastard again and flounced out, slamming the door behind her. He chuckled, trimmed the bed lamp to a faint glow, just in case, and rolled over to catch some shut-eye.

He was asleep within minutes. He didn't dream that night. So he had no idea how long he'd been asleep when he found himself sitting bolt upright in bed, training his .38 on the door.

He saw that it was Vera and lowered the muzzle with a puzzled frown. She gasped and said, "My God, you move fast! How did you do that?"

"Practice. What's *your* problem?"

She said, "I couldn't sleep," as she stepped inside and closed the door after her. He could see by the dim light, now, that she was wrapped in the comforter. He couldn't tell what, if anything, she wore under it. She asked, "Did you mean what you said about not raping me if I sort of took the other side?"

He laughed and said, "I don't *pay* for it, either. You might say I'm a romantic fool. Get in or get out. I'm going back to sleep."

He put his gun away and plumped up the pillows on his side as she moved around the foot of the bed, dropped the comforter to reveal the thin silk slip she wore, and gingerly raised the sheet on her side to slide into bed with him. Then she gasped and said, "Oh, you're not wearing anything? Not even your shorts!"

He grimaced and said, "Sleeping in your underwear is a disgusting habit. But you've still got yours on, so cross your legs, say your prayers, and for chrissake let's get some *sleep!*"

He rolled onto his left side with his bare back facing her and snuggled his head down into the pillows as he shut his eyes. He was just dozing off again when she murmured, "Are you asleep, Dick?"

He groaned and said, "Not now. What do you want, a glass of wawa?"

"It was mean of you to say that other girl had a nicer figure than me. She was short and dumpy, dammit!"

"Okay, you're built like a brick shithouse. Shut up and go to sleep."

"I can't. I've been turning and twisting for hours on that damned lumpy settee and now I seem to be too overtired to fall asleep."

"Speak for yourself, Girl. I could sleep like a log right now, if only you'd *let* me!"

Actually, he was getting an erection, for some dumb reason. But he wasn't in the mood to play games. So he shut his eyes and willed himself into the arms of Morpheus. But now Morpheus was acting like a bitch, too, and it was sort of tough to fall asleep with a throbbing dong and strange stuff just a few teasing inches away from it.

He started counting sheep. But they had hard-ons too, dammit. He tried counting backward from a hundred. Vera was wearing some kind of musky perfume and couldn't seem to settle down. He tried to ignore the way she was rubbing her body around on the mattress next to him. So she gave in first and said, pouting, "I may be a little flat-chested, but at least I'm not *fat*."

He sighed, rolled over, and took her in his arms. She gasped and said, "Oh, you promised you wouldn't get fresh!"

He said, "I'm not getting fresh. I'm just trying to see if you're right. Lessee, you *are* a little flatter topside, but not enough to qualify as flat-chested. I'd call you sort of willowy. Belly's okay and, yeah, I really like them hips."

"Dick, that's enough! Stop right there!" she began. But when he kissed her, and she kissed back, she couldn't say more as he ran his free hand down to cup her silk-sheathed mons in his palm. She moaned and threw her arms around him as he proceeded to rub her silk-filled valley of delight with two fingers. But as they came up for air she protested, "You're going to stain my slip if you don't stop that, you horrid thing."

So he said, "No problem. Let's just slide that slip off so we can do it right."

She said, "Oh, no, I never go to bed naked, even by myself. They say it's wicked. Girls who sleep naked might wind up playing with themselves!"

"Don't worry. *They* don't know what's going on, and if I catch you jerking off I'll make you stop."

She giggled like a little kid being tickled as he got the slip at least around her waist and rolled in place between her naked thighs. But even as she spread them and thrust her pelvis up in welcome the dumb dame had to say, "Please be gentle, Dear. I've never done this sort of thing before."

Her passion-lubricated love maw made a liar out of her as she slid its lips up to swallow him alive. But he was too polite to accuse a lady of insulting his intelligence. Some dames thought they had to talk like that, and her middle-class English accent gave her away as a girl who'd probably been reared by a strict and doubtless frustrated nanny who'd been paid to scare the shit out of her about sex. But obviously old Vera had learned the facts of life from *someone* who'd broken her in pretty good, God bless him, or, more likely, *them*.

As he laid her he kept working the silk slip higher until her naked nipples rubbed against his chest as she kissed him passionately. Vera suddenly grabbed the crumpled silk and pulled it all the way off over her head, sobbing as she said, "Oh, it does feel better with no clothes on, after all. But how shall I ever be able to face you again, after we've been so vile?"

He said, "Let's not worry about it now. I'm fixing to come!"

"Does that mean you're about to have an orgasm, Dear?"

"Something like that. How about you?"

"Oh, women don't have orgasms. We just have to let you brutes have your way with us until you've satisfied your lusts and . . . Could you move a little faster, Dear?"

He did, and said, growling, "This must be really killing you, right?" as she moved her slim hips skillfully and replied, "Oh, I don't really mind, now that I'm getting used to it. Do you enjoy my body as much as you did that awful Costa Rican girl's?"

He said, "There's no comparison." Which was the simple truth. For no two women were the same in bed, bless their sweet hides. She took his assurance at face value and began to move faster, as if to settle the contest in her favor once and for all. So he came in her, hard, and she gasped and said, "Oh, that was mean! I was hoping you'd last longer. Just to be a good sport, of course. It's rather flattering to feel a man wants you, even though . . . Dick, aren't you going to *stop* now?"

"Do you really want me to?"

"Not if it amuses you. I said I was a good sport, and, well, I know I shouldn't say it, but it does feel rather nice and . . . Oh, Dear, what are you *doing* to me, Dear?"

That was a pretty dumb question, even coming from a Victorian English dame. So he didn't answer. He just raised his weight on locked elbows to look down between them as he pounded her to glory. The view inspired him to pound her even harder. For, in truth, Vera was a redhead all over. She moaned. "Wait, take it easy, it's starting to hurt, or at least it's starting to do *something* odd, and if you don't at least slow down I'm going to have to go to the loo or, oh, oh, *Jeeeeeeeeeezusssss!*"

He kept on throwing the blocks to her as she moaned and groaned and rolled her red head back and forth across the pillow, eyes closed and mouth wide open in a silent scream. And then he ejaculated in her still-climaxing vagina and fell limply down against her willowy torso to catch his breath as Vera wrapped her long slender legs around his waist and kept moving and milking until her internal contractions slowly subsided. As he kissed her throat she murmured in a scared little-girl voice, "So *that's* what they meant! My God, I think I just lost my flaming virginity!"

He said, "Come on, Doll Box. You're among friends now."

She laughed sheepishly and said, "I didn't say I'd never *screwed* before. I just meant I'd never seen what all the fuss was about, up until now."

He knew he was in for the story of her life now, whether he wanted to hear it or not. So he dismounted, got out the matches and a claro, and snuggled her against him as he smoked and she talked.

It was funny. Though every dame was different, making love, so many of them told the same old stories. Vera's, in a nutshell, was the one about the girl living in genteel poverty who'd been seduced in her teens by an older friend of the family, found out it didn't hurt, and drifted into hooking as an easy source of income next to working as a lady's maid or shop girl. Hakim's people had found her working Waterloo Bridge in London and recruited her to work for them as an undercover agent who could pass, as need be, for anything from a well-bred Englishwoman to a slut. She confided that she hadn't enjoyed seducing people for Sir Basil much, up until now.

He blew a thoughtful smoke ring up at the bed canopy and asked, "Why did he order you to seduce me, Vera? I wasn't about to take off in that silly skeleton suit, you know."

She giggled, snuggled closer, and confided, "Sir Basil said Sarah and I should do anything to keep you happy until he could have you smuggled out of San José. I didn't know whether I wanted to seduce you or not. You had me confused. I don't know why you made me so uncomfortable before you made me come. Most men are putty in my hands and I can take them or leave them. You seem to feel the same way about most women, and it bothered me. I suppose I was a little jealous, too. That Costa Rican girl was awfully pretty, even if she was sort of plump."

He didn't answer. So she said, "Well?"

"Well what?"

"Am I better in bed than she was?"

He laughed and patted her bare shoulder as he said, "Can't say, yet. We haven't tried all the positions yet."

"My God, aren't you satisfied *yet*?"

"Hell, no, are you?"

"No. Would you think I was awful if I suggested trying what Gaston and Sarah were up to, or down to, when we caught them at it?"

It wasn't easy, but Captain Gringo managed to get at least a little sleep that night, and the night passed all too swiftly, according to Vera. In the morning she served him breakfast as well as more of herself in bed. Then some spoilsport sons of bitches came knocking on the front door with railroad tickets and the sort of chino work clothes engineers and construction workers wore in the tropics if they weren't natives. Gaston could pass for a native or anything else. But Captain Gringo tended to agree that a tall blond guy with Anglo-Saxon features looked a little dumb in a charro outfit and big sombrero. The nondescript sneaks who delivered the tickets and disguises gave the two soldiers of fortune instructions to head for Limón on their own, where they'd be contacted by others with further instructions. Then they lit out, warning Captain Gringo and Gaston not to head for the railroad station until just before the eastbound train was ready to leave.

That left them time to say adiós to the girls right. So everyone went back to bed. Captain Gringo was mildly surprised when he found himself in bed with Sarah, of all people. But as the little blonde stripped off her robe it didn't upset him. It just confused him. He asked, "Who's idea was this, Sarah?" and the little blonde giggled and said, "Vera's in command. We discussed it while you and dear Gaston were chatting with those other men. She was too shy to tell you herself. She's ever so prim, our Vera. But as we're never likely to see you lads again, and there's so little *time*, we agreed there was no sense mucking about with long-winded explanations."

He finished undressing, and as he hauled the smaller, softer Sarah in for a get-acquainted feel, chuckled fondly and said, "I heard you tell her it was true what they said about Frenchmen. I guess I must have disappointed her in that department."

Sarah coyly reached down between them to take his shaft in her smaller, stranger hand, and giggled as she said, "Variety is the spice of life for *us*, too, you know. But, coo, she might have warned me about *this*!"

She was just being polite, he knew, for he'd seen Gaston with his pants off. So he really didn't see what all the fuss was about when he rolled Sarah on her back and entered her. But she seemed to think he expected her to gasp and groan, "Oh, not so deep until a girl gets used to it!"

Then she wrapped her soft arms and stocky legs around him to screw like a little blond mink.

He found her smaller, more well-padded body a welcome change, too, and aside from that, a worry off his mind. The taller, slimmer redhead had said some dumb things during the night, while carried away by passion, and it was good to know the girls weren't going to be pining away for either of them, after all. He wondered why that sort of pissed him off. Sarah was a great little lay, but even as he laid her, the idea of Vera offering her red-thatched snatch to old Gaston right next door made him feel a little used and abused, for some reason. The idea that the tight blond snatch he was in at the moment had been inspired to sex madness by Gaston's skilled tongue just made the whole thing seem sort of dirty, the way a guy liked it, when ships were passing in the dark or, in this case, lamplight.

There was no window in the room. So he made a mental note to keep track of the time as he got to know his new bedroom associate better. Sarah knew they didn't have all day, either. So he'd no sooner come in her old-fashioned than she insisted on getting on top.

He didn't argue. By now he'd have been completely spent, had it not been for the new inspiration of strange stuff. The strange shaft in her inspired Sarah, too. She braced the bare soles of her tiny feet flat against the sheets on either side of his hips and played stoop tag on his love stalk as her big soft breasts bobbed alarmingly in time with her movements. He grinned up at her. She grinned back, dirty, and asked, "Do I screw as good as Vera?"

He said, "I don't know why all you dames want to know that much about each other. I don't *want* to be compared to old Gaston."

She giggled and said, "You're prettier and nicer, this way. But would you tickle my clit, please? For some reason it feels so sensitized this morning."

He reached down to strum her old banjo, politely, but in truth it was getting to be just showing off, or, worse yet, work. There was a fine thin line between a good sport and a slut, and old Sarah didn't have much couth.

He knew he'd never come this way now. So he suggested dog style, and Sarah would have done it in a pig sty, with a pig, he was sure. So they wound up with him standing by the bed behind her where he didn't have to look into her amoral and not too bright eyes as he humped her very pretty rump. He managed to climax that way, at last, after Sarah had come thrice dog style and swore undying love and devotion. He decided to quit while he was ahead. He knew he'd never forgive himself if he'd gotten into anything that nice without coming at least once. But enough was enough.

As the chubby blonde lay face down across the sheets, purring, Captain Gringo sat on the edge of the bed and fumbled for both his pocket watch and a smoke from among the jumble on the bed table. He forgot the smoke as he saw how late it was getting. He patted Sarah's bare behind and said, "I'll see you around the campus, Doll. Gotta grab a whore bath and get dressed."

Sarah answered with a soft snore. He chuckled wryly

and headed for the crapper. That was the trouble with the bitch goddess, Sex. When she offered a quickie, or, worse yet, nothing but your fist, Sex filled your head with endless possibilities. But let a poor guy or gal get a shot at all their fantasies come true and their poor bodies gave out long before they could take Sex up on her offer in full.

There was no tub and the tap water in the sink, of course, was cold. But there were plenty of washrags and towels, so what the hell. He washed and dried and went back to put on the new outfit. He put his money belt on under the khaki shirt and wore the gun rig over it, under the light whipcord jacket. Then he put on the felt hat, picked up the carpetbag the change of duds had been delivered in, and blew Sarah's bare ass a kiss as he went out to the parlor to wait for Gaston.

He didn't have to wait. Gaston was seated on the settee, fully dressed. The Frenchman said, "Ah, there you are, mon sleepy head. Why the luggage?"

Captain Gringo hefted the carpetbag and said, "A guy attracts less attention boarding a train with a bag in his hand."

"Merde alors, what train? We are armed and once more in the money, with a coast of clearness, non?"

"Non. Too many people looking for us here in San José. If Hakim's ruse worked, they'll be looking for us in Puntarenas, too. That leaves the east coast. So get off your duff and let's get the fuck out of here!"

Gaston rose and followed. But as Captain Gringo locked the spring latch of the front door after them, Gaston frowned and said, "I thought we agreed to cross everybody double, Dick."

"Them was the good old days. Last night somebody tried to *get* us, and it wasn't Hakim's people. That makes them even *bigger* bastards in my book. So I think we'd better go along with the bastard we know until we at least figure out who's gunning for us."

They did. Nobody had the railroad station staked out and the train ride down to the jungle-covered lowlands was as uneventful as it was uncomfortable. But by the time two more of Hakim's people had met them at the Limón station and whisked them away to another hideout in the favilla slums above the waterfront, secret-service agent Purvis was getting pensive up in San José. As his assistant, Rumford, entered the office, Purvis said, "Just got a long-distance call from Puntarenas. We've been slickered. Neither Walker nor that little Frenchman were really aboard that train last night."

Rumford protested, "They must have jumped off somewhere along the way then, Sir. My boys tailed them to the station and saw them get on board."

Purvis shook his head and said, "I listen in on other people's telephone conversations. Two British agents did more than follow them to the station. They bought hasty tickets and got on the train after them. They just called Greystoke from Puntarenas and, you think *our* guys are confused? The Brits lost them *aboard* the train! One minute they were there, drinking gin and tonic in the club car. Then they apparently headed back to the coach cars. The Brits finished their own drinks and followed, casually. But guess what, neither seemed to be seated anywhere in the coaches. Greystoke's men looked. In every seat of every coach. How do you like *them* apples, Son?"

Rumford frowned and answered, "Like I said, Sir, they must have jumped off."

"Going downhill, through the mountains, fast, with a sheer drop on one side and a solid wall of whizzing rock on the other? They didn't jump. Both us and the Brits were slickered."

"But how, Sir?"

"Try her this way. What if Captain Gringo and Gaston Verrier never got on in the first place?"

"But we *saw* them board the train, Sir!"

"You mean you *thought* you saw them board it. It was dark. The station is illuminated by faith and a firefly or two at night. Two guys about the same size and wearing the same outfits left the posada we knew they'd been staying in. So everyone assumed they were tailing the renegade and his sidekick. But they were tailing a couple of other wise-asses, who simply changed clothes somewhere on the night train and simply sat down to enjoy the ride with their bare but unknown faces hanging out. I can't *prove* it. But it works better than anything else I can come up with."

Rumford nodded. "Anything else won't work at all, Sir. So what are your orders, now that we've lost them?"

Purvis growled, "Who says we've lost 'em? They're not here in San José, unless my street people lie for no reason. They never went to Puntarenas, so that note Walker left about El Salvador was a crock. He wouldn't have said he was going there if he really was in any case. That leaves what, Rumford? *You're* supposed to think once in a while, too, you know."

Rumford did, and said, "East coast, of course. That's all that's left, and we did pick up that rumor about a mysterious Spanish naval vessel stranded somewhere along the Mosquito Coast, remember, Sir?"

"I remember. It's good to see you've been paying attention, too. So do you really need a diagram on the blackboard, Rumford?"

"Nosir. With your permission, I'll take a team of field agents down to Limón and see if we can locate those rascals again."

"You do that, Son. But be careful. Walker and Verrier are dangerous as hell, as a German agent found out to his sorrow last night."

Rumford frowned and asked, "Where do German agents enter into this case, Sir?"

Purvis said, "I wish I knew. Obviously our boys and the Brits weren't the only ones watching that posada. This morning the local police picked up the body of what they thought was a native cabdriver near the German legation. I took the liberty of staking out the San José morgue, and guess what, about an hour ago, Jager, the kaiser's top Latin American troubleshooter, checked said stiff out for a proper burial. He told the guys at the morgue the guy was related to a Costa Rican cook at his legation and he wanted to do the right thing."

"Naturally he didn't send the dead man to any local undertaker we have on the payroll, Sir?"

"Naturally. We do spread a little cheer among the underpaid help at the morgue. So we know the cabdriver, who didn't have a local coach license, by the way, was shot with a .38. Neatly, between the eyes."

Rumford nodded and said, "The renegade packs a double-action .38 and used to win pistol-shooting contests regularly when he was a troop leader back in the States."

Purvis nodded and said, "So don't let him get the drop on you, and watch out for the throwing knife the

Frenchman carries at the nape of his neck. The next eastbound train leaves in less than an hour. What are you waiting for?"

"Full instructions, Sir. Are my orders to pick them up or just keep them under surveillance for now?"

Purvis said, "By now *they* know what the hell the deal is. So, yeah, you'd better pick 'em up. Alive, if possible. But take no chances."

The reason most of the population of Costa Rica had settled in the highlands to the west was that the coastal lowlands were hellishly hot and buggy. The squalid shacks of the Limón favilla had been thrown together from salvaged crates, palmetto matting, and flattened tin cans and oil drums. There was no street lighting because there were no streets in the favilla. Just a maze of narrow muddy lanes running crookedly between the casually constructed shacks, with a ditch here and there to carry rain water and shit that hopefully floated somewhere else. The resultant stench was enough to gag a pig. But it failed to keep away the flies, mosquitoes, rats, and tropical cockroaches almost as big as rats.

The air was a little better, albeit still eye-watering, inside the hideout the two soldiers of fortune were holed up in, with two sleepy-eyed mestizo gunslicks and an old black crone in one corner who kept cooking plantains and red peppers in deep fat for some reason. No human stomach could have *eaten* such an awful mess. But perhaps destroying the appetites of her temporary boarders was her idea of home economics.

Captain Gringo and Gaston couldn't do much plotting behind Hakim's back with two of his guys in the same one room with them. The mestizos, in turn, answered every question anyone asked them with a sleepy, "Quién sabe?" So it was shaping up to be a long night.

Things got worse when it started to rain. The warm tropic rain on the tin roof didn't cool the air enough to matter but filled the shack with steamroom mist and mosquitoes seeking shelter. Gaston slapped his own face, reflexively, and said, "Mon Dieu, I can't remember when I last spent such a lovely evening." He turned to the old black woman and asked when or if she intended to produce something they could sleep on, hopefully drier than her mud floor. She cackled like a witch and went on stirring her deep fry. Gaston sighed and said, "Merde, that's what I thought. Eh bien, why don't we trim the lamp and just jack off in privacy, hein?"

Captain Gringo told him to shut up and took out his watch. He said, "It's early yet. I think they just brought us here to make sure nobody tailed us from San José." He smiled a question at one of the guys who'd brought them this far and the mestizo yawned and said, "Quién sabe?"

Actually Captain Gringo was right. For, though things were dull as hell in the squalid shack, all sorts of people were up to all sorts of things out in the rain.

Secret-service agent Rumford and his five-man team had no way of knowing just where in the favilla Captain Gringo and Gaston might be, of course. But Rumford was a pretty good field agent, so it had only taken him an hour or so to establish that, since the men they were looking for were not holed up in any of the regular hotels and posadas along the waterfront, they had to be holed up somewhere in the slums of what was, after all, little more than a village.

U.S. secret agents weren't supposed to annoy the local natives if it could be avoided. But could it hurt to move from shack to shack in the dark to press a discreet ear against a paper-thin wall? It was time-consuming as well as soggy work. But Rumford and his men had plenty of time, and plenty of guns, so what the hell.

On the far side of the favilla, another secret agent, named Wolfgang Vogelshorst, had the same idea and a couple more men than Rumford as he carried out the orders of his superior, Oburst Jager of Der Kaiser's intelligence service. Vogelshorst had been told not to come back without Captain Gringo and Gaston, dead or alive. He wasn't as worried about local feelings. People just had to understand that the fatherland had a mandate from a German-speaking Gott. So his team was moving faster, simply barging in on bewildered favilla dwellers for a quick look, a click of the heels, and a move next door.

Meanwhile, Greystoke of *British* intelligence had known for some time about Sir Basil Hakim's way station in the Limón favilla. Greystoke had been trying to put the Merchant of Death in Dartmoor for some time, and it wasn't really all that hard for British intelligence to infiltrate an arms combine based in England. But the team of agents Greystoke had sent had been ordered to proceed with caution and see if they could find out what in the devil Hakim had hired Captain Gringo for before they moved in on anybody.

So as British agents watched the shack and German and American agents moved in on it from north and south, the two soldiers of fortune swatted mosquitoes in blissful albeit bored unawareness of the more serious troubles closing in on them. Gaston said, "It must be getting late. That disgusting mess that disgusting crone is cooking is beginning to smell good. It couldn't be fatal to eat just a *little* of it. *She* eats it all the time, and she must be at least a hundred and ten, non?"

He'd spoken in his version of English. But Captain Gringo told him to watch his big mouth anyhow. One never knew how many languages a lady that old might have picked up in her considerable years on earth. Captain Gringo's stomach was starting to growl, too. But in the end they were saved from having to try deep-fat-fried plantains and peppers.

The packing-case door of the shack popped open, and as the four men inside all went for their guns at the same time, the slim youth in wet poncho and dripping straw sombrero said, "Papadakis sent me. The *Peirene* is ready to weigh anchor and the coast is clear, I think."

Captain Gringo put his .38 away but asked, "Who the hell is Papadakis and what do you mean you *think* the coast is clear?"

The younger stranger said, "Skata, do you want to sail with us or do you want a soapbox lecture? Spyros Papadakis is the skipper of the sponge schooner *Peirene*. I am Kantos, ship's cook and interpreter. What else do you need to know right now? Let's get out of here. My skipper likes to sail with the tide and he has a temper!"

The two soldiers of fortune rose to their feet. The local hired guns didn't. So Captain Gringo knew they weren't going along. This wasn't what was making the hairs on the back of his neck tingle as he said, "You said you *thought* the coast was clear? Run that past me again, Kid."

Kantos shrugged and said, "I spotted someone crouched

behind the shack across the way just now. But it may have just been some native peeping Tom, eh?''

Captain Gringo frowned and answered, ''In this rain? What do *you* think, Gaston?''

Gaston said, ''I think it would be most stupid to leave by the front door when the back wall is nothing but palmetto matting, non?''

Captain Gringo nodded grimly, reached into his pocket, and took out a few coins and his jackknife. He tossed the coins to the old woman in the corner and told Gaston, ''Trim the lamp,'' as he slashed the back wall down one side.

Gaston, Kantos, and the two mestizos thought it was a good idea, but as Gaston plunged the shack into darkness, save the glow of charcoal under the deep fat fryer, the old woman screamed like a banshee and leaped to her feet to stop what she regarded as a shocking vandalism, to hear her tell it.

Kantos grabbed the old woman and held her as Captain Gringo cut an L-shaped flap and said, ''Bueno. Let's go!'' So Kantos dumped the wailing old woman on her duff and followed the two soldiers of fortune out into the driving rain, downslope between other close-spaced shacks.

Behind them, the old woman still rent the soggy air with outraged wails. They weren't the only people who heard her. The German team had worked its way close in any case, and Vogelshorst heard the old woman shouting, ''Damn you, Captain Gringo!'' So he hissed, ''Los, that shack we just saw the peon in that poncho enter! Follow me!''

They did, as Vogelshorst charged the shack, shooting his Mauser with more noise than effect until one of the surprised mestizos still in it cracked the front door, aimed at the German's gun flashes, and blew out the charging German's brains.

His more-cautious followers flopped belly down in the mud and proceeded to smoke up the shack with stolid Teutonic thoroughness. A Mauser slug through the thin front wall sent the old woman headfirst into her deep fat, spilling her and scalding hot grease all over the floor. So the two triggermen still on their feet had hot feet indeed as they charged out, screaming and shooting wildly, one leaving by way of a thin spot in the south wall instead of following his comrade out the front door.

The one who'd charged out the usual exit, bellowing in pain, was of course hit twice before he made it across to the shack in his line of unplanned evacuation. But he was still on his feet and firing ahead of him, dazed from his pain and wounds. So when one of his .45 rounds took a British agent behind said shack in the chest, the Brit he'd just missed growled, "Oh, I say!" and dropped the mestizo in the middle of the path with a well-placed Webley round.

Then he winced and hit the wet dirt as a German, firing at *his* muzzle flash, spanged a bullet off the corner of the shack near his head. So he was more than a little ticked off when another Brit crawled over to him and asked, "What's up, Mate?"

He fired in the general direction of the German team before he replied, "Don't know. But some beggers seem to be *shooting* at us!" So the second British agent, and then the whole British team, was soon pegging shots at the Germans, who of course returned their fire, not knowing what else to do, with their leader dead.

Meanwhile, Rumford and the U.S. secret-service

team had been taught that when in doubt, one should always advance on the sound of the guns. So they were running up the crooked path between the shacks to find out what the hell was going on, when the mestizo gunslick who'd charged out the side wall and may have been a bit overexcited came around a corner, spotted them, and fired from the hip.

Rumford grunted, said, "Shit!" and went down with a .45 slug in his thigh, adding, "*Get* 'em!" even as his men were blowing the mestizo away with their own smoking guns. Then they reloaded and moved on, grim faced and thoroughly pissed, even if they weren't sure why.

It was too good to last, of course. Once the secret-service men charged in to fire at every muzzle flash they didn't know personally, the casualties on all three sides began to get too serious for sensible people to accept. So all three teams began to fight what each thought a strategic withdrawal, dragging their dead and wounded with them.

Obviously, Captain Gringo had a bigger gang than any of them had expected, damn his renegade soul!

The real Captain Gringo and Gaston of course had heard and been somewhat bemused by the sounds of the mysterious firefight behind them as they followed Kantos through the quieter parts of the favilla to the darker end of the Limón waterfront. There, Kantos showed them to a longboat held against the quay by other Greeks manning it. They all piled in. Kantos snapped something that was Greek to Captain Gringo, and they rowed out through the darkness to a big dim shape that might have been a schooner and smelled just awful.

"What's that stink?" asked Captain Gringo.

Kantos said, "Sponge. Haven't you ever smelled sponge before?"

"Sure, but no sponge I ever scrubbed with smelled like . . . let's see, battlefield and cesspool, with spoiled fish thrown in?"

"You'll get used to it," Kantos replied, adding, "The sponges you bathe with are just the soft skeletons of the creatures we dive for. We let them rot until their meat can be rinsed out of the odorless framework, see?"

"No, but I can sure *smell* 'em! How come you guys have to have rotten sponge aboard, Kid? I thought this was really an undercover salvage mission for Woodbine Arms."

Kantos shrugged and said, "It's supposed to be an innocent sponging schooner, too. A sponger that does not stink is not a sponger. Such details can be important, if one meets a nosy patrol vessel, no?"

Captain Gringo had to agree, however reluctantly. At least it was cooler out here on the water, and dead sponges didn't really smell much worse than that old woman's cooking had, once one got over the surprise.

The longboat bumped against a ship's ladder and Kantos went lightly up it, then the soldiers of fortune followed. On deck they were introduced to a burly dark figure who reeked of dead sponge and garlic. Kantos said Captain Papadakis spoke neither English nor Spanish, but they shook hands with him anyway and Kantos said, "Come. I'll show you to your quarters. It's going to be very busy on deck for a while."

It was noisy as well as busy as they followed Kantos

forward to a hatchway. Behind them the skipper was yelling and apparently cursing in Greek as chains rattled, lines were heaved, and so forth. By the time they'd been shown to a tiny stateroom furnished with no porthole and with built-in top and bottom bunks, they could feel the schooner was under way. Gaston stared about in dismay and said, "Merde alors, you call these quarters, M'sieur Kantos? I have spent the night in more than one jail cell more luxurious!"

Kantos shrugged and said, "You should see the crew's quarters, up in the bows. We were told to take good care of you. These are *officer's* quarters, on a Greek sponger. The other people Hakim has on board are no better off."

Captain Gringo asked, "When do we get to meet them, and when do I get to see the weapons Hakim promised?"

Kantos said, "Later. You'll be able to meet the other passengers in the ship's mess, and your machine gun as well as their salvage gear is in the hold, of course. But you'd better stay here quietly until we're well out to sea. I'll come for you as soon as the skipper's good and drunk."

Captain Gringo laughed and asked "Is your skipper in a nicer mood when he's drunk, Kid?"

Kantos replied soberly, "He's never in a nice mood. But when he's drunk he can't hit anything he throws at people."

"He throws things at people? Why?"

"We've often wondered. But the last crewman who asked Papadakis why he had such a vile disposition wound up in the scuppers with a split scalp. I have to go now. *I* could wind up with a split scalp if I don't get back to my galley. I'll send your food to you in a little

58

while. Meanwhile, there's a bottle of retsina in that cupboard by the heads of your bunks. Lock the door after me. The boy I send with your tray will knock once, then twice. Don't open up for anyone else.''

Without waiting for an answer, Kantos left. Captain Gringo sat on the bottom bunk and muttered, "Jesus, what kind of a tub have we wound up aboard?''

Gaston said, "I *told* you I did not want to take this sea voyage.'' Then he opened the cupboard, took out a clear glass bottle filled with amber fluid, and uncorked it, adding, "Eh bien, perhaps it could be worse.''

He took a swig and handed the bottle to Captain Gringo, who did the same, wheezed, and said, "Jesus, you might have *warned* a guy! What is this shit? It tastes like turpentine, for God's sake!''

Gaston said, "It's retsina, or what the droll Greeks regard as wine. It's an acquired taste, as you just observed, but in the legion we learned to drink everything. I've no idea why Greeks put pine tar in their booze and asphalt in their coffee. But they are both strong as the devil. So let's have the bottle back if you're a sissy, hein?''

Captain Gringo took another experimental sip, frowned, and said, "It's not so bad, once you get over the first shock. But I sure hope that Greek cooking on its way tastes more like Mom's apple pie.''

Gaston took the bottle, swallowed a healthy jolt of retsina, and sat down beside him, saying, "This may help if we drink enough first. Greek cooking is something one must be born a Greek to understand, I fear. As a Frenchman, I've never understood why the English like their chocolates and marmalade so bitter. But next to a Greek, an Englishman suffers from a sweet tooth. Wait until you try Greek olives. I think they pickle them in quinine. I have yet to figure out how they manage bitter cheese. But that seems to be the way they like it.''

Captain Gringo tried some more retsina and said, ''Oh well, young Kantos speaks pretty good English, and if he's the cook he might know English tastes. If the others Hakim's sending along work for Woodbine, they're probably Brits, and English marmalade's not as weird as this stuff.''

Gaston took out a smoke as he mused, ''Eh bien, I noticed the slight clipped British accent the boy spoke his English with. What did you think of our young Kantos, Dick?''

''What's to think? He's just a young Greek sea cook who probably picked up his English working in Cyprus or even London, if he's working for Woodbine Arms. He seems like a nice enough young guy. Why?''

''I think he combs his hair on the wrong side. You know what they say about Greek boys, hein?''

Captain Gringo grimaced and said, ''You should hear what they say about *French* boys sometime. Okay, he did seem a little effeminate. But that's not our problem, unless *you* want to bugger him.''

Gaston laughed lewdly and said, ''One imagines our gallant skipper already reams his petite rectum well and très often. That no doubt accounts for the swishy way he walks, non?''

''Don't you ever think of anything but sex, Gaston?''

''Mais non, why should I? It's the only thing that makes existence on this otherwise banal planet worth the time and effort.'' He took another swig of retsina and added, ''Aside from *this*, of course.''

''Hey, you'd better go easy on that booze, Gaston.

You've already put away half the bottle, on an empty stomach, too.''

''Sacre God damn, Dick, when has a Frenchman ever gotten drunk on wine?''

Captain Gringo chuckled fondly and said, ''Many many times, you old goat. I keep telling you and telling you that you just don't have the body weight to drink like a fish, but do you ever *listen*?''

''Of course not. Every time I listen to you I wind up in a gunfight or a war.''

Before the younger American could answer they heard one knock, then two, on the stateroom door. So Captain Gringo rose to open it, and a scared-looking little Greek came in with a tray in each hand. He must not have spoken English or Spanish, since neither worked on him. But when Gaston took his tray as well and said, ''Efcharisto,'' the Greek grinned, nodded, and crawfished out, muttering all sorts of things Captain Gringo didn't understand.

He locked the door again, sat down by Gaston with his own tray, and said, ''I didn't know you spoke Greek, Gaston.''

Gaston said, ''I don't. All I know is that 'efcharisto' means merci beaucoup, the 'kore' is the one who gets on the bottom and the 'kouros' is the one who gets on top, and, oh, oui, 'skata' means shit. That is enough to get laid in Alexandria, if one waves money about as one speaks. I think *that* one was a swish too.''

Captain Gringo didn't care if the galley crew was swishy or not. He was more worried about what Gaston had said about Greek cooking. He dug in, put what looked like scrambled eggs and bacon in his mouth, and said, ''Hey, this tastes just like bacon and eggs. Let's try the home fries. . . . Yeah, they're good too. You're full of shit about Greek cooking, Gaston.''

"Eh bien, I told you there was something sneaky about that Kantos. We may put in at some mainland port on the way to the Bahías. If we do, I vote we jump ship there and quit while we're ahead! Our skipper is an obvious lunatic and the Greek cook can't be a real Greek. Seriously, Dick, I'm really beginning to *worry* now!''

Gaston wasn't the only one who was worried that night. Up in San José, secret-service agent Purvis was burning lots of midnight oil and tobacco as he tried to get a handle on the general confusion. His phone was ringing again. He picked up on the third ring and heard, "Greystoke here, British Intelligence. We need a bit of a favor from Uncle Sam, Purvis."

"Do tell? What can we do you for, Greystoke?"

"Your new battle cruiser *Pittsburgh* is paying courtesy calls at various Central American ports and is due to arrive at Limón within twenty-four hours, right?"

"Maybe. Keep talking."

"Our own RN in these waters is spread a bit thin, and for some reason Whitehall seems to think vessels left over from our French wars suffice to show the Union Jack in these parts. Your cruiser's the fastest thing with guns we could get a message to in time. We'd like to, ah, borrow her for a sea chase."

Purvis laughed incredulously and replied, "I'll bet you would. But the USS *Pittsburgh* wasn't built by the U.S. taxpayers for the Royal Navy, Pal. Who did you say you were chasing?"

There was a cautious pause. Then Greystoke said, "Same chaps you lot are. We've reason to believe Captain Gringo and Gaston Verrier just left Limón aboard one of those ubiquitous Greek spongers. We know for a fact the so-called schooner *Peirene* is faster than she looks. A British subject who should be ashamed of himself saw fit to install a torpedo-ram engine in her when he bought her from her original Greek owners a few months ago. But your *Pittsburgh* should be able to overtake her easily enough."

Purvis frowned thoughtfully and said, "You're still holding out on me, Pal. Walker and the Frenchman aren't wanted by the British government, and *I* know for a fact you guys have hired them to pull some chestnuts out of the fire for you in the past!"

Greystoke sighed and said, "Those were the good old days. They're working for the wrong side now. Actually, we don't want to *hang* your renegade. We just want to *question* him and, above all, *stop* him! He seems to be up to something murky for a peer of the empire who also dabbles in international skullduggery. We're willing to turn those two soldiers of fortune over to you as soon as we're finished with them, of course. But if we don't get cracking, they'll be out of reach bloody soon!"

Purvis growled, "You're all heart. You know we want those guys. But our navy may take some convincing. When did you say that schooner left Limón?"

"Around ten-thirty, on the ebb tide. What difference does *that* make, Old Bean?"

Purvis laughed harshly and said, "You just saved me an argument with our navy department. Walker and the Frenchman couldn't have left Limón aboard *anything* at ten-thirty. At the time in question they were shooting the shit out of a team I sent to arrest them in the Limón favilla. So they're still there, and, come morning and some light on the subject, we'll be sending in some marines from the Limón consulate to do it right!''

There was another cautious silence on the other end of the line before Greystoke said, ''That's odd. Some of our lot was involved in a messy firefight in the same favilla tonight. You don't suppose . . . ?''

''Don't be silly. Our guys tangled with natives, not your guys. Our field agent, Rumford, got a look at the guy who put him on the ground with a bullet in his leg. He was a ragged-ass guerrilla type, like the renegade usually teams up with.''

''Couldn't they have left a rear guard as they headed for the schooner?''

''Surely you jest. I told you they shot the shit out of my boys and chased them clean out of the favilla! We're talking about trained gunfighters, Greystoke. There's only one guy in these parts who could have led such a neatly planned surprise attack, and they call him Captain Gringo. So that Greek sponger's all yours. Unless, of course, you're ready to deal with the cards face up on the table for a change.''

''I beg your pardon?''

''Don't beg my pardon. Tell me what the fuck is going on! I'm not about to stick my neck out and request sea chases at the expense of the U.S. taxpayers until I know what in hell they're chasing, and how come!''

''I told you, Captain Gringo and the Frenchman are—''

''Bullshit!'' Purvis cut in, adding, ''Who do you think you're trying to green? If Walker was smoking up your guys about the same time he was smoking up ours, you know as well as I do he couldn't have been fishing for sponges at the time. You made another slip just now, Buddy Boy. You said that schooner was owned by a British peer. Ergo, you want Uncle Sammy to take the heat instead of you when Queen Vickie gets around to asking awkward questions, right?''

"I assure you, stopping that vessel may well be in the best interests of your government as well as mine, Purvis.''

"So tell me about it.''

Greystoke couldn't, of course. So Purvis said, "That's what I thought,'' and hung up.

Over at the German legation, the officer who'd been listening in on the tapped line didn't hang up. He handed the earphones to his assistant, tore off the top sheet of the pad he'd been covering with shorthand notes, and headed for the office of his superior, schnell!

Oburst Karl Jager was a handsome middle-aged Prussian who would have been handsomer without the saber scar on his left cheek or if he'd at least smiled once in a blue moon. His face wore no expression at all as he took the sheet of foolscap from his underling and read it, leaning back in his severe desk chair behind his severe desk.

He didn't have to have shorthand transcribed for him. Jager could read shorthand, Russian Cyrillic, and, if need be, Arabic. That was one of the reasons Der Kaiser had made him a colonel. The other reasons were that he was utterly dedicated to the German Empire and was a coldblooded killer who made even the bully-boy kaiser a little nervous at times.

Jager put down the paper, stared thoughtfully up at his junior officer, and mused aloud, "Zo! A picture begins to emerge from the mists at last, nicht wahr? Our men were not the only people ambushed in the Limón favilla earlier tonight. Great minds must have been running in the same channels, if both the British and Americans had the same idea of nipping Hakim's plans in the bud. Our men, too, reported shooting at least one native guerrilla, obviously led by this Captain Gringo. Gott im Himmel, such a fighting man he must be! Such a pity he is not on our side. We could surely use such a man when Der Tag arrives!''

His aide saw he was expected to say something. So he nodded and said, ''He and the little Frenchman must be good indeed if they shot their way out of such a situation, Herr Oburst. I can see what must have happened, now. As you say, both the British and Americans were closing in on them as well as us. But of course they must have had lookouts posted and . . .''

''Never mind the past,'' Jager cut in, adding, ''It is the future we must deal with now. Greystoke may be right about the time that Greek vessel left port. On the other hand, he could be wrong. They are not as professional as we are and *we* don't know when the *Peirene* left port.''

He rose and moved over to a big wall map to stare at it with his hands clasped behind him. His aide's balls were itching, but one did not stand at ease around Oburst Jager unless he told one to, and he never did. Jager stared at the map for what felt like a million years to the aide's balls. Then he said, ''They could have waited. Or they could have put in further up the coast to wait for those soldiers of fortune. In any case, we know what the *Peirene* is up to so far from Greek waters, nicht wahr?''

The aide risked a sneering chuckle as he said, ''We always know more than the stupid British and Americans, Herr Oburst. Shall I send a message to have the schooner cut off by one of our own disguised commerce raiders?''

Jager turned, stared at him as if he'd just crawled out from under a rock, and snapped, "Don't be an idiot! If those soldiers of fortune are aboard the *Peirene* it can't be stopped at sea without a fight, and if I wanted it sunk I would not have put my own agent on board. We are intelligence officers, not young Herrs engaged in blood sports, so let us act *intelligent*! If Hakim has those soldiers of fortune aboard for security, it may complicate our plans a bit, but not enough to change them much. Before we do anything about that salvage operation we must let them *find* that wreck for us! Nobody working for us seems to be able to pinpoint it among those unmapped keys and reefs of the Bahías. Hakim may not know where it is either. But if he does, it solves two problems for us. We'll know there's a leak in our navy and we'll be able to salvage that U-boat ourselves!"

He went back to his desk and sat down again, growling, "We still don't know why it went down in that storm. It wasn't supposed to go down in *any* storm. We have to know what went wrong before Der Tag. For Der Kaiser is building a fleet of sister ships for Der Tag and . . . never mind. I am not going to serve mein kaiser sitting here and talking to meinself. When does the next train leave for the east coast?"

"The last midnight train just left, Herr Oburst. There will not be another leaving before morning. But I can send someone over for your tickets right now."

"Don't bother. I always carry tickets. One never knows when such things may come in handy. But I can't wait until morning. Have mein thoroughbred saddled and waiting for me by the time I change into civilian disguise. Wire our agents at Pejivalle and Guagimo to have fresh mounts waiting for me. I see I have some riding to do tonight if I have to take *personal* charge of this unangenehm case!''

So, less than an hour later, a telephone at British intelligence rang, and when Greystoke answered, one of his field agents reported, ''Jager just hit the eastbound trail in mufti aboard a mount that's sure to drop dead if he doesn't slow down between here and Limón, Sir. Do you want him ambushed on the trail by, ah, bandits? We'll never get a better crack at the murderous bastard.''

Greystoke sighed and said, ''No. Alert our people in Limón and let's see if he can lead us to that perishing submarine. Our agents up in the Bahías certainly haven't had any luck looking for the damned thing!''

Aboard the *Peirene*, the rain-soaked chinos of Captain Gringo and Gaston had dried by the time Kantos came to lead them to the ship's mess. The young sea cook had changed to dungarees, a pea jacket, and a wool knit cap. When Captain Gringo asked how their skipper was feeling, Kantos said, ''He's not feeling anything. He's out like a light. But I don't know what we'll do when we run out of ouzo. Papadakis won't drink rum and we're a long way from anyplace we can buy more ouzo.''

Captain Gringo didn't ask what ouzo was. He'd ordered it at a Greek joint back in the States one time. One time had been enough. If retsina tasted like wine laced with turpentine, ouzo was the real thing, pure turpentine, 100 proof. Or maybe paint remover. He'd never swallowed enough to make sure.

They were expecting a salvage crew working for a

British arms firm to be British, of course, so they were surprised to discover that none of the other passengers they were introduced to in the ship's mess were. Hakim had recruited six other men and two women for the soldiers of fortune to guard as they searched for the mysterious Spanish submarine. The head of the team was a German-American naval architect called Keller. One of the dames, the big blond one, was his wife, Herta, a for-real German he'd married while working in Hamburg at one of Hakim's shipyards he probably didn't discuss much with his cardplaying buddy, the Prince of Wales. Keller said he'd worked on American Holland boats, too. So he probably knew his submarines. Second in command was a Hungarian named Horgany. So he'd gotten to bring *his* wife along, too, and she was the little Oriental-looking brunette called Eva, damn Horgany's hide.

None of the others had their own sex lives aboard, assuming they preferred to screw women. Fitzke was a Swiss machinist. Olsen was a Swedish gunnery expert as blond as old Herta but a lot uglier. DuVal was a snooty-looking Frenchman who winced at Gaston's French and said he was up on internal-combustion engines. The last male member of the team, Forsythe, had a British name but was a black Jamaican who knew his way around the Caribbean, he said.

As they sorted everyone out, the scared-looking little Greek from the galley served rum or coffee, depending, to all concerned. Gaston took coffee laced with rum or, to be more accurate, rum with a little coffee in it. Captain Gringo shot him a warning look, but Gaston kept swilling it anyway. Captain Gringo didn't care if anyone else got smashed, but he noticed that while blond Herta stuck to coffee, the Hungarian girl, Eva, took her rum neat. It didn't seem to be affecting her. She looked sort of wild anyway, with those animated slanty eyes rolling around as she tried to follow the conversation in English. Her own English seemed a little fuzzy, judging from her weird accent.

Once they'd all been introduced, the conversation rapidly went downhill. Captain Gringo had hoped someone there could explain more about the wreck they were searching for. But nobody seemed to know much more about it than the soldiers of fortune did. So he asked Keller, "Is this trip really necessary, if nobody knows where the effing wreck *is*?"

Keller shot a look at the Jamaican, Forsythe, who said, "We'll find it, Mon. We already got it narrowed down to one of the uninhabited islands. For I got friends and relations on Roatán an' Bonacca and they'd know was they a shipwreck *thereabouts*. They sort of *in* the wreckin' business, when the fish ain't biting, you see."

"All too well. But isn't there another main island, Forsythe?"

"Sure, Utila, closer to the Honduran coast. Ain't got no contacts there. Old Honduran government too picky about black folks lighting beacons on a stormy night. But that Spanish sailor boy wasn't picked up near Utila. They fished him out of the water amongst the bitty uninhabited keys further out. Before he passed away he say he didn't make it far from the place his ship run aground, see?"

Gaston stared owlishly over the rim of his cup and said, "Mais non, there *are* no uninhabited islands among the Bahías, mon ami."

So the big Jamaican shrugged and said, "Shoot, Mon, I hope you don't consider no-good Nigger-Caribs *people*! You gotta have *people* on a key for it to be *inhabited*, right?''

Captain Gringo said, ''Whatever Black Caribs are, they're there. Do you savvy their dialect, Forsythe?''

''Hey, Mon, I'm *civilized*, even if I do have a healthy tan! Nobody savvies Carib, Black or otherwise, Mon. Do you meet a Carib, the first thing you has to do is shoot him in the head to gain his undivided attention! Nobody can talk to Caribs. It's been tried. Those crazy Caribs ain't ones for conversation. They shoot strangers on sight.''

Keller cut in to say, ''We've gone over all of this before, Walker. The plan is for you to man the machine guns, trained on the shore, as we cruise just out of arrow range, searching each key in turn for some sign of the wreck.''

''What if it's under water?''

''We have diving gear, if it comes to that. I don't see how a vessel that size could be completely under, since the coral flats between the islands are shallow. If it did find a hole to settle into, there should be plenty of black oil staining the white coral sands of the nearest key, see?''

''If you say so. The salvage end ain't my job. Did you say machine guns, plural?''

Keller nodded and said, ''Hakim had us load two Maxims aboard with the other gear, along with plenty of ammo. You don't have to worry about that *now*. They're stored safely in the hold until we need them.''

Captain Gringo put down his coffee cup and said, ''I need 'em now. Can you show me the way, Kantos?''

The young Greek looked surprised but nodded and replied, ''If you wish. But we're nowhere near the Bahías yet.''

He rose and said, "Yeah, and I want to check 'em out and mount 'em well before we get there. Coming, Gaston? You'll have to man the stern gun, you know."

Gaston looked up, bleary-eyed, and asked, "Is someone calling my name in vain?"

So Captain Gringo said, "Never mind. Let's go, Kantos."

They left the mess and moved forward along the companionway. Kantos had just pointed out a ladderway leading down to the hold when a door on the other side of the companionway slid open and the burly Papadakis popped out. Kantos sighed and muttered, "Skata," as the skipper grinned owlishly, grabbed the young Greek, and dragged Kantos back into his cabin, struggling and protesting in Greek.

Captain Gringo followed the uneven match into the skipper's evil-smelling stateroom, and as Papadakis wrestled Kantos to a bunk stained with vomited booze and worse, he asked mildly, "Are you in trouble, Kid, or just acting coy?"

Kantos gasped. "The animal is trying to *rape* me, dammit!"

So Captain Gringo shrugged, moved in, and rabbit punched the big Greek across the nape of the neck.

It didn't work. Papadakis let go of his first victim and stood up to turn with a bearlike roar as his bloodshot eyes focused on Captain Gringo. Then he growled deep in his throat and grabbed for the American who'd love to have tapped him for some mysterious reason. Papadakis didn't just *growl* like a bear. He was strong as a grizzly and not nearly as nice as he proceeded to slam Captain Gringo against the door jamb over and over again, obviously most annoyed but oblivious to the punches the big Yank was throwing, even as they tore hell out of his blind-drunk face!

There had to be a better way. Captain Gringo kicked Papadakis in the crotch as hard as he could. The monstrous Greek grimaced in pain, but hung on and slammed the now dazed American against the wood again. So Captain Gringo growled, "Oh, shit," drew his .38, and shoved the muzzle deep in the big Greek's paunch as he pulled the trigger.

That worked better. Papadakis stared sadly at him from his ruined face, tried to say something, and let go to fall backward like a redwood cut off at the roots. He hit the floor with more noise than the muffled shot had made. Captain Gringo slid the door all the way shut behind him before he shook his head to clear it and asked Kantos, "What happens now?"

Kantos sat up on the bunk, stared soberly down at the big corpse between them, and murmured, "Now we both die. You don't understand my people. He was our *captain*!"

"Oh, for God's sake, the drunken brute just tried to sodomize you, Kid. Don't you have any rules at all in the Greek merchant marine?"

"Yes. One rule is that the master's word is law, at sea. The others hated him as much as me. But we Greeks are an inflexible race, and there is only one way to deal with mutiny at sea, so . . . "

Captain Gringo put his head to the closed door a moment before he said, "I get the picture. But, so far, this is still our little secret. Nobody seems to have heard that muffled shot."

Kantos shrugged and said, "What of it? It's only a question of time before he's found, and everyone knew how he's been after my body, so . . . "

"So shut up and listen, Kid. The rest of the crew knows he had a serious drinking problem, too. Guys who stagger around drunk aboard a ship at sea sure fall overboard a lot, don't they?"

Kantos gasped and asked, "My God, do you think we can get away with it?"

Captain Gringo said, "We'll have to, unless we want to do some swimming ourselves before morning. You go first and see if the coast is clear. Trim the companionway lamps as you lead us to the nearest way up on deck. What are you waiting for, Kid? *Move!*"

Kantos did. They got away with it. As the dead skipper went over the lee rail and hit with a soft splash amidships in the shadows of the moonlit sails, someone aft called out in Greek, albeit casually, and Captain Gringo hissed, "Don't answer! If the helmsman doesn't put about, and puts it together later, he'll feel too guilty to speak up. Let's get down to the hold fast. That's where we're supposed to be right now, remember?"

Kantos nodded and led the way down to the hold ahead of the engine-room bulkhead. It was dark, of course, until the young Greek struck a match and lit a hanging lamp that helped a little bit. Captain Gringo had to find the arms and ammo himself amid the other stored gear. But he managed. The two machine guns were packed in petroleum jelly, bless Hakim's heart, and aside from being spanking new as well as rust free, the headspace had been set right, for a change. He grinned and said, "One thing you gotta hand the old gunrunner. He knows his guns. *Now* what's the matter?"

Kantos was leaning against a nearby packing case, crying like a frightened girl. Captain Gringo put a comforting hand on the shoulder of the rough pea jacket and said gently, "Hey, look, it's *over*, see?"

Kantos sobbed, threw both arms around Captain Gringo, and kissed him passionately on the lips. Even worse, it felt good!

The big American shoved the little Greek away, gasping. "For God's sake, Kid, I thought you didn't go in for that sort of thing! I know *I* don't!"

Then he saw what had happened when the force of his shove had knocked off the other's big knit cap. As he stared in wonder down at the heart-shaped face staring up at his adoringly from between raven's wings of long black silky hair, he blinked and gasped. "For God's sake, Kid, are you one hell of a convincing fairy or a real girl?"

Kantos looked just as surprised as she asked, "Didn't you *know* I was a woman, Dick? I didn't try to hide it from you. I just thought you considered me plain, until you saved me from Papadakis!"

He laughed like hell and said, "I'd have hit him harder had I known what he was *really* after! But that male costume had me sort of confused, Kantos. Is that a Greek girl's name, by the way?"

"Kantos is my family name. My first name is Antigone. Don't you *want* to kiss me . . . Dick?"

He did. It felt a lot nicer, knowing their first thrilling kiss hadn't meant he was starting to get strange, and as he held her closer, leaning against the packing case, it seemed impossible that he'd ever thought the body under the pea jacket was that of a sort of soft-looking boy. The thick wool still left a lot to be desired, though, so he started to unbutton it for her as they tongued each other and made nice nice. But she stiffened and said, "Not down here, Dick. What if someone should come?"

Coming was just what he'd had in mind. But he said, "Yeah, we'd better get these guns topside and mounted under tarps before we take our pants off. Do the other crew members know you're really a girl, Antigone?''

"Of course, although it would be cruel of me to wear skirts at sea where the wind blows so much. But even Papadakis respected me, when he was sober. Back on Kríti—you call it Crete—my male relatives have a certain reputation for dealing harshly with anyone who insults their kinswomen. So now that you have saved me from Papadakis, my virtue is safe once more.''

"Oh, hell, *there* went a great notion!"

She laughed and said, "*You* don't have to worry about my virtue, Dick. You are not a Greek from Kríti, see?''

He wasn't sure he did. But the next hour or so kept him too busy to worry about the social customs of Greek villagers, as they mounted machine guns fore and aft. Nobody argued about the nails they drove into the deck up by the bows. But as Captain Gringo got to work on the stern gun, the sleepy-looking helmsman back there asked Antigone in Greek if they'd cleared all that hammering with the skipper. She assured him they had and rather cleverly added that Papadakis was up in the bows at the moment, if the helmsman wanted to clear it with him. The Greek at the helm repressed a shudder and said no thanks. So they lashed a tarp over the securely mounted Maxim and went to Antigone's cubby near the galley to see her etchings or whatever.

She didn't have etchings to show her newfound friend, but as she undressed in the little one-bunk chamber by soft lamplight she reminded him not a little of the marble nymph her much uglier schooner was named after. But as he enveloped her white flesh in his arms there was nothing cool as marble about her, and when she pulled him down on the bunk and spread her creamy thighs in welcome, there was something a lot yummier than a fig leaf between them.

As he entered her she gasped in delight, then sighed. "Oh, God, I'm *really* in trouble now!"

That was enough to cool a guy some, even amid such lovely warm surroundings. He said cautiously, "Don't you know how to, ah, take care of yourself, Antigone?"

She wrapped her soft white limbs around his waist to hug him deeper as she smiled up at him adoringly and said, "I didn't mean *that* sort of trouble, Darling. Heavens, I'm a sea cook, not a blushing virgin. It's just that I was hoping *one time* would be enough to, ah, thank you properly."

"You didn't have to thank me this way, Kid. I'd have hit him even if you really had been a boy."

She giggled and moved her hips teasingly as she replied, "I'm so glad I'm not. It's been a long time since I've enjoyed this sort of thing, discreetly, and I can feel *you* haven't had a woman for some time either, true?"

He started moving in her faster as he said, growling, "Let's save the pillow talk for later, huh?"

So they did, and it was wonderful. Despite Gaston's jokes about Greek loving, Antigone needed nothing odd or acrobatic to enjoy sex in a healthy peasant fashion, and, with her moving under him so nicely, Captain Gringo found all the inspiration he needed to keep going as they made old-fashioned earthy love, climaxing together over and over until by wordless mutual consent they stopped to get their second winds.

She sighed and said, "That was lovely, dammit. You make love the way I always imagined the elder gods atop Mount Ida must have done, back in the Golden Age."

"You'd make a pretty good fertility goddess, too, Antigone. So what's to *damn* about it?"

"I'm going to want *more,* of course. But now I know there's no way I'll be able to get all I want of you."

He kissed her and smoothed her black hair across the pillow as he chuckled and said, "No problem. Both the other women on board are married, so I'm all yours, Kitten."

She sighed and said, "It's not that simple. We'll have to be very discreet. I told you some of the crew are from my village back on Kríti, and if my people ever found out . . ."

"Okay, we won't tell anybody we're lovers. Who's to know if we don't do this on deck a lot?"

She sighed and said, "We're not completely safe even here. Oh, Dick, if only we could be alone together on some desert island, instead of risking our reputations like this aboard a crowded little schooner!"

He sighed and said, "I usually get to have this conversation by the cold gray light of dawn, around Monday, with luck. Are you saying this has to be a one-night stand, Antigone?"

"If only I had that much strength." She sobbed, kissing him in sudden passion and groping for his semierection to guide it back where she wanted it.

But after they'd come again she said, "You know I can't resist you. So you'll have to be strong for both of us."

"I wish you'd make up your mind, Kid. I can be strong as hell, once I know what a lady *wants*!"

She sobbed. "I want you inside me every waking minute, day and night, but we have to be discreet about it. We don't dare risk this *every* night. What if we agreed to only try to get away with it every *other* night?

That way, one of us could make a point of being with someone else when the crew knows the other is in his or her quarters alone, see?''

He laughed and said, ''Okay. Who do you suggest I sleep with when I'm not sleeping with you, the blond German dame or the little spooky Hungarian?''

She didn't have his sense of humor. She sank her nails in his buttocks as she pulled him deeper in and said, ''If I catch you looking at another woman, now that you're mine, I'll feed your liver to the sharks, Darling!''

She sounded like she meant it.

It took the crew almost until noon the next day to notice their skipper was missing, and not miss him all that much. After some debate it was decided he must have fallen overboard in one of his drunken fits and that the first mate, Venezis, was automatically their new skipper.

Passengers as well as crew found Ilias Venezis a vast improvement over the late Papadakis. Venezis was a calmer, smaller, older man who'd been running the *Peirene* most of the time in the first place, and now that he was in full command, he seemed able to do so without hitting anyone. Better yet, Venezis spoke a little English as well as a smattering of Spanish. So the Jamaican, Forsythe, could get through to him when they were approaching a reef.

There were a lot of those along the east coast of Central America, but the big Jamaican was fantastic at spotting them well before the lookout up on the main mast could. The jovial Jamaican explained that in his

day he'd met most of the reefs of the Caribbean personally, with a keel, and so he knew all too well what it
meant when the whitecaps ahead seemed to be running
against the prevailing trade winds from the northeast.
Venezis told his helmsmen not to argue with the big
black when and if he yelled at them to give the
schooner hard right rudder. So the next few days passed
serenely enough, save for a few close calls when the
Jamaican was eating or taking a crap.

The nights were more fun for Captain Gringo and
Antigone, or at least every other night was. She'd
weakened the night following their first get-together.
But after screwing him silly while bitching all the while
about her reputation, she was adamant about him spending every other night with Gaston, who probably found
it just as boring.

With nothing to make love to but his fist and a bottle
of rum, Gaston was enjoying the voyage less, and
bitching about it more than Antigone was.

Captain Gringo wasn't in the habit of discussing his
conquests. But Gaston had things figured out, once
he'd seen Antigone at mess in a tight seaman's pull-
over. The others on board had of course known earlier
that their sea cook was a lady in pants. Gaston said he
admired Captain Gringo's taste and asked him what she
tasted like. Captain Gringo told him to find his own
stuff to eat, and Gaston said, "Merde alors, if only one
could, aboard this stinking species of tub! But the big
blonde seems devoted to her damned husband, and the
wild-eyed Hungarian creature has been très difficult to
get alone."

They were having this conversation in the privacy of
their tiny stateroom, of course, as Antigone had said no
that night. The schooner was sailing through the dark-

ness with the sails reefed and the engine just ticking over, dead slow. Forsythe had to sleep sometime, too.

Captain Gringo let Gaston rave on as he played with himself in the top bunk until the horny Frenchman said, "I'm sure the Hungarian girl is hot for adventure. She shows the whites of her eyes très alarmingly, considering her Oriental eyes."

Captain Gringo growled, "Keep it down to a roar, you old goat. The bulkheads are thin, and her husband, Horgany, is a lot bigger than you."

"Merde, not where it counts, I'll bet. That little Eva is gushing for a good lay, I tell you. Aside from being perhaps a bit taller than me, Horgany drinks too much for a man who means to keep his woman satisfied."

Captain Gringo snorted and said, "Shit, Gaston, nobody aboard this tub's been drinking more than you!"

"That's different. I have not been called upon to keep it up for that little Hungarian spitfire. Besides, you are wrong. I have only been *trying* to stay drunk. Horgany drinks himself into a stupor every night before going to bed with all that ooh-la-la! It's a crime against nature, I tell you!"

Captain Gringo thought about that as he lay naked under the sheet in his bottom bunk. He had thought he'd picked up a few bedroom glances from little Eva at mess that night, and, yeah, Horgany had been socking his booze away pretty good. But he told Gaston, "You'd better stay true to your fist, anyway. Lots of dames flirt just for practice, and we have enough problems now. Speaking of Hungarians, isn't Hungary part of the Austrian Empire at the moment?"

"Oui, but what has that to do with my poor frustrated cock?"

"I'm trying to figure out how come we've been sent to spy on German naval architecture with so many guys who speak German. Keller is a Yank who's spent most of his adult career in Germany. Horgany's a subject of the German-speaking Hapsburgs. Fitzke says he's Swiss. But he's from the German-speaking part of Switzerland even if he is."

Gaston shrugged and said, "What of it? Olsen, DuVal, and Forsythe are not Boche, and it stands to reason Hakim would want people who can read German dials and so on, non? Besides, the species of international death dealer has arms factories in Germany as well as England, non?"

"Yeah, if there's one thing I admire, it's loyalty. How far in the future do you figure that big war Der Kaiser seems to be arming for gets to start, Gaston?"

"If my French countrymen have anything to say about it, twenty years at the most. We still owe the Boches for 1870, and *next* time..."

"Yeah, I figure the Brits will get into it too. So where will that leave Hakim, if he doesn't screw himself to death first?"

"Very rich, of course. That is why he wants to know how Linke-Stettin underbid him. He obviously intended to build submarines for *everybody*."

Captain Gringo frowned and mused aloud, "I wish I knew if we were doing the right thing, dammit. My own country's liable to get into it, if it's a big enough war, and I'd hate to think I helped Hakim if one of his underwater gunboats ever sinks a Yankee ship!"

Gaston laughed and said, "Who says either of us will get to live long enough to find out? If we make it to the end of this century, I, for one, will be astounded. Besides, if Hakim can prove his rival's submarines are no good, Spain will stop buying them, and a Spanish-American war seems a lot more likely, in *our* time, non?''

''Yeah, but what if *Hakim* starts building underwater gun buckets for Spain? He will, you know, if they ask polite.''

''Mais oui, but you forget how slowly the gears of Spanish government turn, Dick. If you Yanks don't finish off the Spanish Empire within the next few years, you're not as seriously annoyed with them as young M'sieur Hearst would have one believe. If the Spanish navy is forced to change its plans, it will take them at least ten years of très tedious discussion. I agree Hakim is a treacherous toad. But in this case he may be on the side of the angels despite his satanic tendencies.''

Captain Gringo yawned and said, ''We're talking in circles. But what the hell, we've gone along with the game so far, and even if we had a crystal ball, who'd listen to a couple of guys like us? Let's get some sleep.''

He closed his eyes and tried to. Then he stared up at the creaking mattress between them and muttered, ''Oh, for God's sake, Gaston, can't you do that when I'm not sleeping under you?''

''I do. Is it my fault I am more passionate than your cautious Greek girl friend? If I do not keep this damned thing satisfied it tends to get me in trouble. I have never gone in much for sodomy, but that mess attendant, Socrates, is starting to look better to me every time he bats his big brown eyes at me!''

Captain Gringo laughed despite himself and said, ''Socrates? Is that the little Greek boy's name?''

''Oui. Worse yet, he speaks a little French and says he loves me. So if you don't want me getting merde all over my adorable dong, just leave me alone and let me satisfy it less disgustingly!''

Suiting actions to his words, Gaston proceeded to jerk off harder. Captain Gringo wrinkled his nose, sat up, and pulled on his pants. He knew he was probably being puritan, but it still smacked of homosexuality to him to share a stateroom with a grunting and groaning jerk-off artist. So he decided to enjoy a smoke on deck while Gaston enjoyed himself.

The moon was high and the sea was calm and phosphorescent as he moved up into the bows on his bare feet. The trades were gentle and clean-smelling, albeit a little cool against his bare chest. But he wasn't uncomfortable enough to go back down for his shirt. He'd only brought one cigar topside. If Gaston wasn't asleep by the time he finished it, he'd just have to knock out the crazy son of a bitch.

He'd moved to the bows to avoid the effort of conversation with the night watch, aft. He didn't think it was true about *all* Greek boys. Save for little Socrates, most of the crew seemed masculine enough. But trying to make small talk with guys who didn't speak English or Spanish could be another kind of pain in the ass.

So he was a little annoyed when he found someone else up in the bows, leaning against the waist-high forward cabin. He tried to remember what Antigone had said was Greek for ''howdy.'' Then he saw it was Herta Keller, the big German blonde. So he said, ''Gut aben,'' and she laughed and said, ''It's Guten abend, Dick. I thank you for the thought, but perhaps we'd better stick to English, nicht wahr?''

He laughed too and said, ''Yeah, you would have heard more English than I've heard German, married to a Yank.''

Herta looked away and asked, "Why is the water shining so? I have seen phosphorescent waves in European waters, of course, but never so bright as this. The sea looks as if it were on fire all around, nein?"

He moved over to the mounted machine gun and checked the lashings of its tarp as he said, "Yeah, some nights the waves are bright as hell. But let's not talk about it. It stirs up bittersweet memories of a lady who wrote poetry about green liquid fire and all that poetic stuff."

"That sounds like the sweet part, Dick. What was the bitter? Did she say no?"

"She said yes. Then she got killed in a fight she had no part in. I said I didn't want to talk about it."

He was tempted to go back below. He could see that she was as bad as Gaston when it came to talking. But she was a lot prettier, and he'd just lit a claro, so he moved over and rested his buttocks on the cabin coaming next to hers instead. As he did so, the schooner heeled a bit and placed his hip bone closer to hers than he'd intended. She didn't move away. So he stayed where he was.

There was a moment of awkward silence. Then he said, "I understand your husband worked for Hakim in Hamburg."

Then it was her turn to look away and ask, "Do you have to talk about *him*? Oh, look, a shooting star! I wonder if we both just made the same wish, Dick."

He sort of wondered, too. But he said, "I've a reason for asking about what you guys were doing in Hamburg, Herta. Hakim says his rivals built that mystery sub at Kiel."

"So?"

"So how come he knows so much about Linke-

Stettin's shipbuilding techniques if he's never worked around 'em?''

She hesitated, then said, "If you must know, my husband did once work for Linke-Stettin in Kiel. They fired him, of course. Sooner or later they always fire him. So now we find him working for a degenerate named Hakim, and is not a life of travel and adventure wunderbar?''

She didn't sound like she meant it. He said so. She shrugged and said, "When we married I expected him to take me to America. If I had wished to stay in Germany I would have married a German.''

She shuddered and added, almost to herself, "Gott, if only I'd met a nice Russian, or even a Turk. But that is what one gets for guessing wrong.''

He said, "You're right. We'd better not talk about your old man if you're ticked off at him." But then he couldn't help asking, "What happened, Herta, did you two have a little spat this evening?''

She made a wry face and said, "We never fight. We have an understanding. But, Gott im Himmel, with a *boy*?''

"Holy Toledo! You have to be kidding! A man would have to be nutty as a fruitcake to pass up something as nice as you for . . . uh, it's not *Socrates,* is it?''

She sobbed and said, "Who else? That's how he lost his job with Linke-Stettin. That's how he always loses his jobs with real men! He says variety is the spice of life and that I must understand he really loves me in his own way. But, Gott im Himmel, how would *you* feel if your husband made love to other men, Dick?''

He tried not to laugh as he said, "Pretty weird. I'd feel funny being married to another man even if he *didn't* cheat on me. I feel for you, but I just can't reach you, Herta.''

She took one of his hands, placed it in her lap as she spread her thighs under her thin cotton skirts, and asked calmly, ''What if I *help* you reach me, Dick?''

He was reaching her pretty good. His questing fingers could feel the moistness of her aroused or vengeful vagina as he held her closer with his other arm but said, ''Hold it, we've got some ground rules to work out here, Herta. You're a married woman and I'm . . .''

''Oh, for God's sake, while you're acting coy my husband's locked in our stateroom with my male rival for the night! Don't you *want* me, Dick?''

''I wouldn't want you to think I was a sissy, too. But what if your old man gets excited about the cruel things you're doing to my hand?''

She lay back atop the cabin as she rubbed his hand harder between her thighs and asked, ''Who's going to tell him?''

He said, ''*You*, for openers. I'd be a liar if I said I didn't want more than a feel, Herta, but I've been around this block before, and the one thing you can count on when a woman cheats on her husband for spite is that she's sure as hell going to let him know about it sooner or later.''

She started pulling up her skirts as she insisted, ''I said we had an arrangement. He says it's all right for *me* to seek variety too, the brute. Naturally he knows I don't like girls. But he never so much as said I couldn't join him in his mad passion for men, so what are we waiting for? Stop teasing me, Dick. I want it *now*!''

He knew she was going to be just as pissed and just as likely to get him in trouble with her husband if he rejected her at this late date. So he stood up, got between her bare chunky knees, and dropped his chinos to enter her, standing, as he held her spread legs like wheelbarrow handles. She gasped and pleaded, "Not so deep! Let me get used to it first, for Gott's sake. It's been so long since I've had a real man in me and...Ach, nein, forget what I just said and *do* it, Liebling!"

So he did and, thanks to Antigone, was able to do it right. Aside from being rested and not a little frustrated by the Greek girl's on-again-off-again ways, the contrast between the big chunky German blonde and the dark petite Antigone served to inspire him to new heights. But as soon as he'd made the frustrated Herta come, of course, she started getting cold gray thoughts and said, "Nein, not again. Not here on the open deck! What if someone should come?"

"We just did. But you may have a point. Let's see, we can't go to your place and we can't go to mine so...Oh, sure, Socrates has a cubbyhole of his own next to Antigone's and we know *he* won't be using it tonight, right?"

She blanched and asked, "Do you really think I'd let you lay me in that disgusting sodomite's quarters?"

"Why not? Your husband's laying him in *your* quarters, isn't he?"

Herta laughed, told him how awful he was, and then they pulled down her skirts and pulled up his pants to go somewhere they could do it right.

As they locked themselves into the mess attendant's perfumed cubby, he lit the lamp and cautioned her, "No conversation. His boss, the cook Antigone, is right next door and we wouldn't want to give her a bad impression of poor Socrates, see?"

Herta managed not to giggle too loud as he dropped his pants again and helped her undress by soft lantern light. As he got his first good look at the buxom blonde in the buff, it was as if that first quickie up on deck didn't count. For if Antigone, next door, had the body of a petite marble nymph, this one was built like a Wagnerian soprano made of angel-food cake with lemon frosting.

She fell back on the fortunately fresh sheets the fussy fairy had made his bed with earlier that evening and welcomed him with open arms and legs as his raging erection found its way home again through the familiar blond brush. They went deliciously crazy together for a time, and though they tried to keep the moans of passion down to a roar, they must not have been as quiet as they'd hoped, because they suddenly heard a dainty fist pounding on the bulkhead and then they froze as Antigone, on the other side, cursed them roundly in Greek.

It got worse. As they lay entwined in each other's flesh, they heard the Greek girl next door get up, stomp on her sea boots, and them slam her own door as she moved out to the companionway. The next time she knocked and swore, it was on the cubby door they'd entered through and, hopefully, locked right!

"Don't answer!" Captain Gringo whispered as Antigone kicked the door with her sea boots and yelled something awful through the panel in Greek. Despite herself, Herta giggled. On the far side, one feminine giggle probably sounded much like any other, so Antigone spat, "Skata!" and stomped off in a huff.

Herta said, "We'd better get dressed and get out of here schnell!"

But he said, "That's the sure way to get caught. We don't dare open that door until she's back in her own quarters, see?"

"What if she's going to tell her captain on us, Dick?"

"I don't think she is. But if she is, we're no worse off in the end. The odds are better on getting caught if we try to sneak out now after all the hell she just raised out there. Let's just enjoy life while we wait for things to simmer down."

"I am too nervous now to make love! What will you do if the captain comes to that door, Dick?"

"Tell him to go away, of course. He speaks English and I don't think he's married to Socrates."

"Mein Gott, that might make him think you, too, are like mein husband!"

"Yeah, well, better me than you. We haven't tried it dog style yet, Doll. Or would you rather get on top?"

She laughed a little wildly and said, "This *is* pretty funny, once one thinks about it, nicht wahr?"

He didn't think it was going to be funny if Antigone figured out who was in there. But he grinned back at the big blonde reassuringly and said, "You wanted to play dirty tricks on your old man. So let's get dirty some more."

She said, "All right." Then she rolled over on her stomach, placed a pillow under her to raise her rump invitingly, and said, "Let's pretend I am a Greek boy, too."

He frowned down at her heroic rear and said, "I thought you said your old man was the one who went in for that sort of thing, Herta."

She said, "He is. I've never let him put it in me that way. So I'll *really* be cheating on him if I give myself to you that way, ja?"

"I think I grasp your logic, sort of, but I'm not sure

this is such a good idea, if you haven't done it before. They tell me it's sort of an acquired taste, Herta.''

"Who told you, boys or girls?" she asked archly as she arched her spine and reached down with both hands to spread her cheeks for him.

He didn't answer. He heard movement next door and knew Antigone had come back from her snit. He didn't want Herta sounding off again. So he got above and behind her, spit on two fingers to lubricate her anal opening, and eased it in the naughty way as Herta groaned and said, "Gross Gott!"

"Hush! Do you want me to stop?"

"Nein, it feels . . . interesting, now that I have gotten used to it and, ach, ja, do it do it do it!"

He didn't have to do much, and now he knew she was full of shit, as well as cock, about never having done it that way before. Nobody moved like that unless they liked it a lot, and he had it on good authority, albeit all female, that nobody liked it that much back there the first time.

But what the hell, he'd known she was a cheat from the beginning, and it was sure a change, so . . . Then the skipper pounded on the door and yelled at them in Greek, which was all Greek to Captain Gringo, save for the name, Socrates, which old Venezis seemed to be cussing hell out of.

Captain Gringo knew he was in a hell of a mess whether he answered or not. So he just kept buggering Herta to get at least a last good orgasm out of an otherwise dismal mess. Then someone else shouted in Greek, farther away, and Venezis shouted something that must have meant "Just you wait!" before he ran off down the companionway. Captain Gringo smiled in pleased surprise and ejaculated in Herta as, next door,

Antigone tore out of her own quarters again. Herta pleaded, "More, more, deeper, Dick!" But he said, "Save it for a rainy day, Doll. We're never going to get a better chance to get out of here now. I'll hit the light and go first. Haul on your duds and don't follow me unless the companionway is clear. It should be. Every-one seems to be up on deck for some reason. So that's where *I'm* going, too!"

He pulled up his pants, put out the lamp, and cracked the door to see if he was right about the companionway being empty. It was. So all he had to do was find the nearest ladder and go up on deck. When he did so, he saw that everyone was crowded in the stern. So that's where he went, too, calling out, "Hey, Gang, what's up?"

Antigone grabbed his bare arm and hauled him closer to the taffrail, saying, "There, back along our wake. Where in the devil have you been, Dick? I just looked for you in your stateroom but Gaston said you'd just left."

"Had to go potty. Let's not worry about that now. I have to get the tarp off that *Maxim,* dammit!"

He elbowed his way through to the stern gun, shouting, "Everybody but the helm forward and take cover, dammit! Don't any of you know a coastal pirate when you see one?"

As the others at least started giving him some elbow room, Venezis said, "My lookout's been watching it for some time, Captain Gringo. It just began to move closer a few minutes ago."

Captain Gringo stripped off the tarp and armed the Maxim, growling as he said, "He should have given a holler sooner. Vessels in these waters are supposed to show running lights, unless they're up to something sneaky.''

''*We* are not showing our running lights, Captain Gringo.''

''That's what I just said. Get everybody *forward*, dammit! They're closing fast and you're not supposed to wait until you're in range before you duck, see?''

''We are cruising at reduced speed and they are not closing too fast. What if I ordered full speed ahead, Captain Gringo?''

''In the dark, in uncharted waters off a lee shore? No thanks, I'd rather take my chances with the dangers I can see. Hey, Forsythe, you anywhere in this crowd?''

The big Jamaican joined him at the taffrail to ask what he wanted. Captain Gringo pointed the way the jacket of his Maxim was aimed and said, ''You know these waters. What the fuck is that chasing us?''

Forsythe squinted and replied, ''Hard to tell in this light, Mon. But it's too small for a gunboat and coming up our wake too fast for a sailing craft.''

The mystery vessel bounced over a wave through a patch of brighter moonlight and the Jamaican said, ''Hey, you know what that is, Mon? That's a *sea sled*, that's what that is, Mon!''

Captain Gringo almost asked a dumb question. Then he remembered seeing something about sea sleds in some magazine and said, ''I thought those newfangled speedboats only raced in quiet waters.''

The Jamaican nodded and said, ''They supposed to. I saw one flip like a flapjack in Kingston harbor when they had a race there last year. But till it flipped it was beating every other craft in the water, Mon. I suppose a mighty good helmsman, in a mighty good hurry for some mighty good reason, could skip a sea sled across the high seas did he have to. That boy coming up our wake must be either crazy or *good,* Mon!''

Captain Gringo squinted through his machine-gun sights as he frowned and said, ''It's a sea sled all right, but it's *not* going full speed. It's just cruising, not planing, and Venezis is right that we could outdistance it easy.''

Forsythe said, ''Not did it open up full throttle, Mon. That fool back there is playing some sort of game with us. You mean to shoot it up?''

''I can't, yet. It's just out of range and, yeah, hanging there, the son of a bitch. How many passengers could you cram in a sea sled, with guns?''

The big black shrugged and said, ''Six or seven at the most. I don't see *nobody* aboard that funny notion. Unless they're all down on the duckboards. Mon, that sure is a crazy way to go to sea!''

Above and behind them, they heard the masthead lookout shout in Greek. Captain Gringo called out to anyone who was listening to tell him what that was all about, and Antigone came over to kneel at his side and explain, ''Nikos, aloft, says he thinks there is yet another vessel on the horizon, astern. He makes it a topsail schooner and it, too, shows no running lights. Oh, look, the funny little boat is gaining on us now!''

Captain Gringo swore and snapped, ''Forsythe, grab the wheel and heel us as close to a right angle as you can get!''

''Which way, Mon, windward or alee?''

''Just *do* it! That son of a bitch coming up our wake isn't full of guys, it's full of *dynamite!*''

Forsythe could take a hint. The big Jamaican made the helm in two bounds, took the wheel with one good shove that put the startled Greek crewman on his duff, and gave the *Peirene* hard right rudder to use the trade winds as well as the engine to whip her bows to the west as, up the wake, now doing at least thirty-five or forty knots, came the light sea sled some wise-ass out of range was steering by *Marconi control*!

"Skata!" Antigone gasped. "You've put us broadside to that thing!"

Captain Gringo snapped, "Hit the deck and stay there," as he opened up with the machine gun. He didn't aim directly at the guided missile. It was skipping wildly across the chop at the very limit of its stability now, as its distant controller opened its throttle to full speed. So he fired at an angle for it to cross while, up in the bows, Gaston at the other Maxim did the same, drawing an X of white water for the sea sled to cross.

It didn't. As its scowlike plywood bows entered the crossfire they were treated to a moment of mock sunrise as the explosives-laden craft evaporated in a big ball of fire. Then they all got wet as the explosion lashed the *Peirene* with salt spray and soggy splinters.

Antigone laughed incredulously and asked, "How did you know Gaston was manning the other Maxim, Dick?"

He said, "He had to be *some*place and he wasn't *here*. Stay down. The sons of bitches are sending another one at us!"

He held his fire as he watched a second sea sled tear out of the darkness toward them like an enraged water beetle. It was moving even faster as the wise-ass manning its Marconi controls steered it zigzag in an attempt to outwit his aim. But, as Forsythe had observed, a flat-bottomed sea sled could only press its luck so far on the open sea. Just as it got within maximum range it hit a whitecap wrong, bounced high in the sky, and rolled over twice in the air before landing upright on its flat bottom with a mighty splash; then it tore off to the west across the curved wake of the *Peirene* as Captain Gringo put some plunging fire into it for luck.

Then, as the sea sled began to act like a water beetle indeed, he laughed and called out, "Forsythe! Hard right rudder and full speed ahead. We'd better get out of here poco tiempo!"

Antigone said, "It seems to be circling out of control now!"

He said, "Yeah, so let it circle all it wants. That other vessel's not about to come any closer with that toy as likely to hit *them* as us!"

The big Jamaican at the helm didn't want to discuss it. He just signaled the engine room full speed and, as the schooner's powerful screw began to churn green fire in the phosphorescent sea, swung her bows north to put some distance between them and the mystery ship on the southern horizon.

So in less than an hour they seemed to have the moonlit Caribbean all to themselves again. But Captain Gringo stayed at the stern gun anyway until Antigone whispered, "You're soaked to the skin, Darling. Would you like to come to my cubby and get warm? I don't think anyone will notice in all this confusion."

He smiled wistfully and said, "*We* would, if another sea sled exploded against the hull while we were, ah, getting warm. I thought you said we had to be discreet, Honey."

"I know, but I'm feeling weak again. I should be ashamed of myself, but that damned little Socrates has

96

a man in his cubby next to mine and I just know I'll never get any sleep tonight anyway!''

He smiled innocently and said, ''That does sound disgusting. Do you know who's in there with him?''

She said, ''No. I thought he was the only one like that aboard, now that Papadakis has, ah, fallen overboard. But we've been at sea for some time and, well, I know how *I* feel right now!''

He said, ''Me too. Maybe later, when things settle down. We shouldn't have our heads together like this, if you really want to be discreet. Now that we seem to be in the clear, people are starting to pick themselves up off the deck and, oops, heads up, here comes Venezis.''

She quickly rose and moved away as the new skipper joined Captain Gringo at the taffrail and said, ''The lookout says that other vessel has vanished. Should we slow down to leave less of an illuminated wake?''

Captain Gringo said, ''Not just yet. The phosphorescence fades pretty fast.'' Then he called to Forsythe, ''Hey, Jamaica, do you think you could swing us shorewards into the mangroves without running us aground?''

Forsythe swung the wheel as directed and called for reduced engine speed as he said, ''The odds are fifty-fifty with the seas on fire tonight. The Good Lord has lit a lamp unto my feet and I ought to see the shallows before I hit 'em. It's dangerous ahead no matter which way we steers now. We should be just south of the Mosquito Keys by now. So we'll likely run aground before morning anyways!''

Captain Gringo grimaced and said, ''*You're* a cheerful son of a bitch!'' Then he turned to Venezis and added, ''It's your ship, Captain. Any objections?''

Venezis said, ''Of course not. Between you, you

seem to have saved us from a watery grave. But would you mind telling me what in the devil we are doing now?''

Captain Gringo said, ''We can't risk full speed ahead at night in waters like these, phosphorescence or not, and those sea sleds move like spit across a hot stove. The last time those other guys saw us we were heading up the coast. If we put in and duck our masts behind some mangroves . . .''

''Ah, I see the plan, and I like it. But I heard the Indians along the Mosquito Coast are, ah . . .''

''Savage is the word you're groping for, Skipper. They are. They have good reason to be. But they probably won't bother us if we don't bother them.''

''What if they do?''

''That's why Hakim sent Gaston and me along. They probably won't. The Mosquito Indians don't go looking for trouble like Caribs. They just don't much like to work on sugar plantations for no pay. So they tend to shoot and run. But how deep in solid ship's timbers can a reed arrow penetrate, right?''

Venezis said *he* was sure a cheerful son of a bitch and moved forward to herd everyone who didn't have good reason to be on deck below, out of the way.

Gaston thought he had good reason to be on deck as he moved aft to consult his younger comrade. He said, ''Eh bien, since only our adorable ass end is exposed to danger at the moment, I put a fresh belt in the bow gun and came back to see if you have any idea at all what is going on, my noisy youth.''

''Did you put the tarp back on?''

''Mais non, I thought the hot Maxim would *enjoy* salt spray. Who do we think launched that dramatique whatever at us back there, Dick?''

Captain Gringo frowned and said, "I'm still working on that. I can think of lots of people who might not want us looking for that sub."

Gaston spat over the stern and said, "In that case my money is on the Boche. They have always loved surprises. The Prussian needle gun came as a très dismal surprise to us back in seventy."

Captain Gringo nodded and replied, "I hope that *was* a German getting cute back there. It makes me feel better about the square heads we have on board."

Gaston shrugged and said, "Keller's the only real Boche aboard and he's half-American as well as queer, non?"

"How did *you* find out about him and the rosy-cheeked Greek boy?"

"Socrates came running out of Keller's stateroom as I popped out of ours. We were both buttoning our pants at the time. I think he was more embarrassed than me. But he was lucky as well. Keller's wife just missed the show, coming along the companionway just a moment later. I still haven't figured out who *she* was screwing when things got so exciting. I feel a little jealous."

Captain Gringo muttered, "Heads up," as Keller himself moved back to join them. Captain Gringo said, "Evening, Keller. Didn't the skipper order everyone below just now?"

Keller said, "He did. I'm still in command of this expedition. What in the hell is going on? I was still getting dressed when I heard that huge explosion."

Captain Gringo said, "Marconi-controlled sea sled, converted to a fast floating bomb. Were they working on anything like that when you were working in Germany, Keller?"

"Not exactly. But of course they were experimenting

with wireless. The idea was invented in Germany just a few short years ago and . . . You say they were steering explosives at us with it? That's crazy. Not even Marconi can send radio waves more than a few miles yet."

"I know. That's why we have to stay a few miles away from those pricks. You'd better stay below with your wife, Keller. The next thing that comes out of the dark at us could be a reed arrow, poison tipped."

That seemed to do it. As Keller left, muttering to himself, Gaston sighed and said, "Such a waste. All that blond femininity to enjoy and he prefers sissy derrieres. Who do you suppose could be getting some of that real stuff, Dick?"

"Jesus, don't you ever think of anything but pussy?"

"Mais non, I told you I didn't go in for sissy boys. At least, not up to now. But sacre goddamn, if I don't get some of the real thing soon . . . Oh well, I see Socrates is taken. I wonder if he's the only one like that aboard."

"Don't try to find out. Despite the jokes about Greek boys, most of them are just as likely to bust your head for stealing a feel as anyone else."

"Oh, I don't know. Where there is smoke there should be fire, and we know at least one Greek boy aboard lives up to the reputation, non?"

"One's about average in any crowd this size. The poor Greeks are stuck with all that garbage Plato wrote. They tell me Plato's required reading at a lot of boys' schools all over. So behave yourself."

Before Gaston could reply, Forsythe called from the helm, "Mangroves ahead!" and signaled dead slow. The two soldiers of fortune leaned over the starboard rail to see what looked like a line of fuzzy inkblots with their roots in green fire as Venezis rejoined them and

told the Jamaican he was running them aground, God
damn it. Forsythe laughed and said, "I know what I'm
doing, Mon. But I don't talk Greek. So stick around
and have your boys drop anchor when I gives the word,
hear?"

They were still arguing about it when Forsythe steered
the schooner between two clumps of mangrove and
snapped, "Now!"

So a few seconds later they were swinging about on
the anchor chain as Forsythe cut the engine and the
Peirene came to a dead stop with her stern shoreward
and her bows aimed seaward between the mangrove
clumps. Captain Gringo said, "Nice going. You're a
pretty good seaman, Jamaica," and Forsythe said, "Good?
Hell, I'm the *best*, Mon!"

The rest of the night passed uneventfully. They were
too far out to really have to worry about natives on
shore, but they kept a deck watch anyway. Captain
Gringo didn't take Antigone up on her invitation, even
when most of the ship turned in before morning. For
one thing, it wouldn't have been delicate until he'd had
a bath. For another, he was up the mainmast for the
next few hours, trying to see if he could spot that other
vessel out to sea.

He couldn't. So as the empty seaward horizon
began to turn pearl gray he turned the lookout over to
one of the crew members to slide down the stays and
enjoy an early-morning skinny dip before turning in
to catch a few winks, alone, as Gaston watched the
shoreline.

It seemed he'd barely dropped off before the little

Frenchman woke him to report they were standing out to sea again and ask if he wanted to do anything about it. So he got up and went on deck as Gaston turned in. There wasn't much to see. The trades were blowing a fog bank in off the open sea, and the Greek who'd relieved Forsythe at the helm didn't speak English or Spanish. So he went to the ship's mess to see if there was anything to eat.

There was. Most of the others were sitting at the table as Socrates served them, looking sort of shy. When someone called out Captain Gringo's name, Antigone stuck her head out of the galley, looking hurt. Herta Keller sat sipping her coffee as if butter wouldn't melt in her mouth.

As he sat down, Fitzke, the Swiss, asked if they were out of danger now, and Captain Gringo said, "No. We won't be out of danger until this job is over. But if we don't run aground amid the Mosquito Keys this morning, we ought to be okay until this fog lifts."

The little Hungarian girl, Eva Horgany, rolled her spooky eyes and asked him just where they were. So he said, "Almost halfway to the Bahías. We still have to round the big bulge of Cape Gracias a Dios, where Nicaragua and Honduras bump borders. I hope the fog holds up past there. The channel between the cape and the offshore Half Moon reefs is a favorite hunting ground for coastal pirates and patrol boats."

Eva gasped. "Will those patrol boats be looking for *us*?"

He shrugged and replied, "Hopefully they'll be more interested in the pirates. That's how come they're patroling those waters. Nobody's supposed to know about *us*, see?"

She still looked worried. Keller looked worried too as he said, "*Somebody* else knows about us! Have you figured out who tried to stop us last night, Walker?"

Captain Gringo shook his head and said, "Not really. I think we can eliminate the American or Royal Navy. No ironclad would have had to act so sneaky against a soft-hulled schooner. So that other craft was probably a souped-up sailboat, too. After that it gets tougher. I doubt if either the Spanish or their German friends really want us to salvage that wrecked submarine ahead of them."

Fitzke lowered his cup and said, "That means *they* haven't located it yet either, no?"

Captain Gringo nodded and said, "That's another thing we've got to worry about. I mean, how come? The Spanish must have known they'd lost a vessel among the Bahías well before anyone else did. So why haven't they or their German pals already found it? Has it occurred to any of you we could be on a snipe hunt?"

Some of the Europeans looked blank. But the German-American Keller knew what a snipe hunt was and objected, "The Hondurans fished a Spanish submariner out of the water near the Bahías, dammit."

Captain Gringo shrugged and said, "So what? They didn't see any submarine, did they? What do we really *know* about that soggy Spaniard anyway?"

Keller said, "I read the official report. Hakim was able to get a copy for us from a Honduran officer who enjoys good cigars. I forget the shipwrecked Spaniard's dago name, but he said he was an oiler aboard His Most Catholic Majesty's D-Uno. Hakim says the D stands for 'Debajo' and Uno, of course, means—"

"I know what it means," Captain Gringo cut in, adding for those who spoke no Spanish, "It would be U-One in Der Kaiser's navy. Hakim told us it was the first submarine the Spanish bought. I'd still like to know if it was really wrecked at all. That submariner could have been a plant, you know. I doubt if Spain really wants Uncle Sam to know it has at least one functional underwater gunbucket cruising anywhere close to Cuba these days, and anyone can lie if he's told to."

Keller said, "Dammit, the man *died* shortly after the Hondurans rescued him. He couldn't have been faking it. I read his medical report. He'd been in the water for some time, clinging to some wreckage. Aside from exposure, he was coughing blood a lot. The Honduran navy medics assumed that he had pneumonia. Hakim says it's more likely he inhaled some chlorine before he got out. *That* smells like a wrecked submarine too."

Captain Gringo frowned and said, "I know what chlorine smells like. But what in the hell would chlorine gas be doing aboard a submarine?"

Fitzke said, "I can answer that. Sea water spilled on storage batteries filled with sulfuric acid generates chlorine. So Keller and Hakim must be right about the vessel hitting hard enough to crack her hull. If a man in the engine room got out, it couldn't have been from far under. So the submarine has to be aground somewhere, awash or not too deep."

Captain Gringo shrugged and said, "Yeah, and not even Bo Peep can find her. There's a piece of the puzzle missing, folks."

Little Eva said, "If someone has already found the

wreck, would be they trying to stop us from looking for it?"

He'd figured she was smart. Even her husband seemed surprised but not displeased by her suggestion as he said, "By God, she's right! How far did you say we were from those Bahías, Walker?"

Captain Gringo said, "At least two days. And everyone else has had a chance to search among the Bahías a lot longer. So forget a conning tower still above the surface like a sea serpent, gang. Even if it lay fully submerged but visible from the surface, somebody should have *found* it by now."

Keller said, "Not if it's tucked in some cove the way we were last night."

"There's a law saying other search vessels can't poke into mangroves, too?"

"Not if they're deep-draft naval vessels. Why did you think Hakim sent us aboard this shallow-draft sponger?"

Captain Gringo thought as he sipped some coffee. Then he nodded and said, "Maybe. But that sure makes the other guys dumb as hell. Any gunboat that doesn't carry lifeboats smaller than this schooner is in big trouble in these waters!"

He put the problem aside in favor of his ham and eggs and let the others worry about it for now. Hakim wasn't paying him and Gaston to find the wreck. They just had to keep these other idiots from getting killed before *they* found it or, more likely, gave up.

He finished and went back out on deck to enjoy a smoke in the fog. As he moved up in the bows, Herta Keller caught up with him and said, "Dick, we must talk."

He looked aft, past her, and said, "Well, it's too foggy for anyone to spot us from more than a few feet away, but can't it wait until dark, Honey Box?"

She sighed and said, "Nein. It is about what happened in the dark we have to talk about, Dick. I don't know what got into me last night."

He just smiled crookedly at her. She blushed and said, "Aside from you, I mean. I was terribly annoyed with mein husband, but I may have made a mistake. When I went back to our stateroom I found him all alone, and that Greek boy *is* the one who delivers food and liquor, as mein husband said."

He saw no reason to play tattletale. So he just shrugged and said, "I'm glad you made up, Mrs. Keller."

"Please don't be angry, Dick. I shall never forget what a grand time we had together, but despite our troubles, I am still a married woman and, well, if he's not having an affair with anyone else on board, I don't see how we can continue with *ours*, do you?"

He tried not to look as relieved as he felt as he nodded soberly and said, "No. We have to consider the children, right?"

"Silly, we have kein kinder. I told you last night I knew how to take care of meinself and . . . Are you mocking me, Dick?"

"No. I'm mocking me. I get the picture, Herta. Maybe I'll see you around the campus sometime, okay?"

She didn't get that, either. But she kissed him in a disgustingly sisterly way and left him to field-strip and clean the forward Maxim in peace, and feeling a lot better than she'd found him.

He'd just finished and lashed the tarp over the machine gun when Antigone joined him alone in the bows.

There seemed to be a lot of that going around this morning for some reason.

The petite Greek girl looked shyly aft, threw her arms around him to give him a far from sisterly kiss, and asked, "Why didn't you come to me last night, you brute?"

He pointed at the covered machine gun and said, "I was sort of busy."

She laughed and said, "It's just as well. In all the excitement, more than one crewman passed my open door to find my bunk chaste and pure. I heard some of them laughing just now about poor Socrates. I fear I was not the only one who heard him entertaining someone next door to me last night. Naturally, none of the others will admit it was he. So it's the talk of the ship, and if we are very very discreet . . ."

"What time do you want me to drop by, Sweet Stuff?" he cut in.

She fluttered her lashes and said, "Not to my quarters. It's too dangerous, with everyone trying to catch Socrates right next door to me. I took some bedding and pillows down to the hold just now. There's a crate of ship's stores I had almost emptied and, well, now it *is* empty, and discreetly lashed in a corner with the only opening facing the bulkhead and . . ."

He cut in again to say, "I admire a lady who thinks on her feet about her ass. I'll come to you by moonlight, though hell should bar the way, or unless someone sinks us first."

She giggled and asked, "Would you like to see our love nest now?"

He said, with a wistful smile, "Hold the thought. This damned fog's lifting and someone could need me on deck in a hurry."

"But you promise to come tonight?"

"Honey, I promise to come *all* night, if we live that long."

They did, but it wasn't easy. The fog thinned out within the hour and, when it did, the lookout, topside, spotted steamer smoke to the northeast and called it down to Venezis, who swore and called for reverse screw. Captain Gringo shook his head and said, "Steady as she goes, Skipper. If they're over the horizon to us we're over the same to them, and we're not throwing smoke, thanks to internal combustion."

Venezis spat the right orders in Greek, but asked in English, "What if it's one of those fast new Yankee torpedo rams?"

"We'd sure better hope it doesn't spot us," Captain Gringo replied, adding, "All sorts of ships are patrolling the Half Moon reefs over that way, Skipper. We're never going to make it around the bulge if we duck every smoke plume in these parts. The idea is to get around to the west as soon as possible so there'll be fewer to duck!"

"I don't like this at all," Venezis protested, looking all about as he added, "It's too fine a day to be sailing such waters. That damned sky is clear as far as the eye can see and the damned horizon line is sharp as a razor in every direction. There's no way for a patrol boat to miss a shark fin against the skyline right now!"

He was right. The lookout called down in Greek. Venezis said, "Skata!" and whirled to stare back along their wake. Captain Gringo turned too, to watch the dark lateen sails coming their way from the southwest and observe laconically, "Yep, that's a coastal pirate, sure as shit. They can drop that rig flat in less than a full minute. I told you that patrol boat's smoke plume was too far out to worry about. Our chums back there must have just put out of the mangroves to see what kind of goodies we might have aboard.''

Venezis said, grim faced, ''I know what that other vessel is. Our Aegean Sea scum use the same Arab rig. What are you waiting for? You still have your machine gun covered, dammit!''

''Simmer down and order full speed, Skipper. We ought to be able to outrun 'em without a firefight. I'd just as soon not have one with something bigger patrolling the same waters just out of sight but maybe not out of earshot. The wind's hardly blowing right now and the sounds of gunshots carry pretty good over water, you know.''

Venezis ordered full speed ahead. It soon became obvious that wasn't doing them much good. The Greek skipper stared aft and said, ''I don't understand. You're right about the light airs. So how is that goddamned lugger moving so fast? Lateen sails are fast, but not *that* fast!''

Captain Gringo said, ''Obviously they have an engine, too, and a good one. They're just using their sails to hold them steady on one heel as they overtake us. It's a pain in the ass to have to aim a deck gun with said deck rocking under you a lot, see?''

''I see all too well what they intend! Shouldn't we put our own canvas up for the same reasons?''

''No. We don't have deck guns to worry about. So let the pricks guess which way we're about to yaw when they get within range. I can aim a Maxim from any angle and with bare poles we'll be more maneuverable than them.''

Gaston came aft to join them, rubbing his eyes as he muttered, ''What is going on, Dick? I just awoke to

find us tearing madly at full speed through the chop."
Then he spotted what they were looking at and said,
"Merde alors, I thought the Royal Navy had cleared
this stretch of the Mosquito Coast."

Captain Gringo said, "That was last year. There
seem to be some new kids on the block. From the way
they're moving, they don't look like the usual native
fishermen turned rogue. That tub has a mighty good
engine in its hull. Internal combustion, too. They're not
throwing steam-engine smoke."

Gaston said, "Oui, they must take their profession
très seriously. I'd better get up to the bow gun, hein?"

"Not yet. See how they're holding their position well
out of gun range?"

"Oui; they obviously don't intend to move in on us
until we're both clear of that gunboat smoke I now
regard to seaward. As I said, they must be professionals
who know their chosen trade."

Venezis said, "Oh, God, I told that damned Papadakis
I did not wish to come to America!"

Captain Gringo said, "Relax. Gaston and me are
pros, too. If you have to do something while we wait
'em out, make sure none of the others pop out on deck
uninvited. It could start getting sort of noisy around
here before too long."

The skipper made the sign of the cross and moved
forward, leaving them alone with the sweating but
silent helmsman, who probably only knew half of what
was going on. Captain Gringo said, "Damn. I should
have told him to get Forsythe. We may need a man at
the wheel I can talk to."

Gaston said he'd go get the Jamaican. But he didn't
have to. Great minds seem to run along the same
channels, and the big black came around the cabin

coaming to call out, "Skipper says we got more trouble, Mon. What's up?"

Captain Gringo pointed at the lateen sails behind them and told Forsythe to see for himself. The Jamaican whistled and said, "I know that lugger, Mon. That's old Providencia Pete and the centerboard lugger, *No Quarter*!"

"Is he a friend of yours, Jamaica?"

"Providencia Pete ain't *got* no friends, Mon. His mammy hated him so much she kept dropping him on his head when he was a chil'. That boy is one mean nigger, and he feeds his crew on rum and gunpowder, too!"

"Okay, if he's looking for trouble he came to the right place. Take the wheel and when he moves in we'll give him some crossfire, too."

"Won't work." Forsythe sighed, adding, "That old boy ain't just mean. He's smart. He may not know about the machine guns, but he won't close within range of small arms anyhow. Soon as we don't have that smoke plume over yonder, Old Providencia Pete means to open up on us with his deck guns. Rifled breech-loading two-inchers, long range. You mind do I make a suggestion? It's sorty of sneaky."

"By all means, Jamaica. *I* sure don't have an answer for long-range deck guns!"

Forsythe explained how it was the custom of those who knew the pirate and his customs to hoist a white flag and start tossing presents over the side to him. Half the time, if Providencia Pete was pleased with the results, and the endangered vessel kept going, he'd give up the chase. The pirate knew he could always overtake his victims again if they tried to satisfy him with cheap trade goods.

Captain Gringo started to ask what they had on board to toss over the side to the pirates. But Gaston said,

"Mon Dieu, could anyone I know still be that innocent? You take the wheel, Forsythe, I shall prepare the tribute for our Jolly Rogers, hein?"

So, less than two hours later, with the smoke of the distant patrol boat no longer haunting the horizon to seaward, the *Peirene* hoisted a pillow case and slowed down as the grinning Gaston heaved what looked like a sea chest over the stern and let it trail aft on a long line. But as the *No Quarter* moved closer, the sponger edged away like a nervous virgin, staying just out of range as the pirate skipper laughed and called out to his crew, "I told you they was sissies. But keep that deck gun trained on them anyway, whilst we see what they think their white asses is worth."

The *No Quarter* reversed its screw as it bore down on the bobbing sea chest and a crewman leaned out over the side to haul it aboard with his gaff hook.

He didn't. Aboard the *Peirene*, Gaston sparked together the bare copper ends of his improvised battery line, and the sea chest, along with the pirate lugger, *No Quarter*, dissolved in a fireball of exploding dynamite!

As the shock wave passed over the schooner, Venezis stared in wonder at the falling debris and said, "By the beard of Pantocrator, it worked! Shall we see if there were any survivors?"

The two soldiers of fortune just looked at him, and he said, "Sorry. Dumb question, once one thinks about it."

It was good to be home again in a sweet old-fashioned girl as Captain Gringo lay with Antigone in her improvised love nest down in the hold that night.

112

She'd been right about it being what she called discreet. He'd never have thought to look between the nondescript packing case and the bulkhead, even if he'd expected to find someone playing slap and tickle down there in the dark.

The inside was fixed up soft and comfy with the pillows and bedding she'd smuggled from her quarters, and, even better, by bracing his bare feet against the inside of the crate he was able to put it to her deep as hell with those two pillows under her sweet little derriere. She said she liked it, too.

They couldn't smoke between times. Aside from the danger of someone wondering why they smelled tobacco smoke coming from a deck vent, it was already stuffy enough down there. Before holding their naked bodies, the packing case had been stuffed with coffee and goat cheese. Gaston had been right about Greek cheese being an acquired taste. But Antigone smelled just right as she rubbed her perspiring naked flesh against his, so what the hell.

He'd already established that she liked her loving old-fashioned, albeit often. So he didn't suggest anything acrobatic, even if it had been possible in such close quarters. He was glad he hadn't when, during a pause for pillow conversation and, hopefully, renewed inspiration, Antigone snuggled close and said, "This is nice. But I'll be glad when I can use my real bunk again. It should be safe tomorrow night, Darling. Nobody is watching Socrates next door now. They've found out who he's been doing you-know-what with."

He grimaced and said, "Remind me never to make love to Socrates behind a keyhole. Who'd they catch him with?"

"You'll never guess. It's that Swiss, Fitzke."

He blinked in the dark and said, "You're right. I never would have guessed it was *him*!"

She shrugged a bare shoulder against him and began to fondle him as she said, "Well, the poor Swiss doesn't have his own woman aboard, like Keller, Horgany, or you. But it's still a little disgusting, don't you agree?"

"I've never tried it. What happens, now that the crew knows?"

She frowned and asked, "What do you mean, Darling? Nobody's going to *do* anything. They just wanted to *know*. My people are a curious race."

"You can say that again. On some vessels the skipper would maroon anyone caught at buggery, it they let the poor bastard live at all. Your people must be tolerant as well as nosy."

She chuckled and said, "Everyone enjoys gossip. But Greek men feel it is beneath them to pick on weaklings, unless their *women* are involved."

"Hmm, that makes them not only regular guys but explains a lot of dumb stories, I guess. How come your people are so strict with you girls if they don't mind a guy getting sexy with another guy?"

"Heavens, can't you see the difference, Dear? What you and I are doing would be a *sin,* if my father ever found out. What Socrates does is just *silly*! The poor thing thinks he is a woman, but it's not his fault he's crazy. That Swiss is the one who's disgusting, as well as weak. Could *you* put this in such a disgusting place, Dick?"

"Heaven forfend!" he answered innocently, adding, "I'd cut it off first."

She laughed and said, "Please don't. I'm not through

with it just yet." Then she stiffened in his arms and hissed, "Oh, someone's coming!"

It sure wasn't him. He stiffened, too, and tried not even to breathe as they heard someone moving around in the hold outside. Moving *sneakily,* too!

A million years went by as the two lovers in the crate listened with bated breaths to the odd rummaging sounds outside. Then whoever it was went back up the ladder and shut the hatchway quietly.

He took a deep breath and muttered, "Must have been one of the crew, swiping a late snack or something."

But Antigone said, "No. In the first place, not even Socrates would steal ship's stores. That *would* get a man killed aboard a Greek vessel! Besides, he didn't come over this way, where the provisions I haven't unpacked yet are."

"He or she was surely after *something* down here, and I don't think it was sloppy seconds, no offense! We'd better get dressed and get out of this box, Doll."

"Don't you want to make love to me some more, Darling?"

"Want to. Can't. I have to see if I can find out what he she or it might have swiped. Aside from that, this hold isn't as private as you said it was, and I do so hate to get caught with my pants down!"

It was a good thing he'd thought of that. They'd barely dressed and lit the hold lamp to examine the cargo when the hatch above slid open and Venezis called down, in Greek. So when Captain Gringo told her to for Pete's sake answer and let him take it from there, she did, and the skipper came down the ladder, holding a big belaying pin in his free hand and wearing a puzzled frown on his leathery face.

Captain Gringo said, "You heard it too, eh? Your cook

here just told me she thought someone was trying to get into her stores. But when we came down just now, whoever it was was gone."

Venezis went right on frowning thoughtfully as he said, "You heard noise in the hold and came down alone, without calling *me*?"

Captain Gringo opened his jacket to expose the grips of his .38 as he answered easily, "I didn't come down alone. I told this girl here not to follow. But you crazy Greeks all seem to want to act brave for some reason."

Venezis said, "All Greeks *are* brave, even our women, as you just saw. But you probably just heard something shifting as we tacked just now. The trades are picking up again and I've hoisted the sails to save fuel, see?"

Captain Gringo certainly didn't want the skipper poking about among the packing cases. So he said, "Well, everything seems secure enough now." Then he turned to Antigone and said briskly, "You did well to tell me anyway, Miss . . . Antigone, right?"

She managed not to laugh as she demurely admitted that was her name. So the three of them went back up out of the hold together and, what the hell, he'd seen enough to know that none of the other cases had been broken into. So maybe it had been someone just looking for a place to jerk off or something.

But he told Gaston about it anyway as he rejoined the Frenchman in the stateroom he was supposed to be spending the night in and now, dammit, had to.

Gaston didn't like it. He said, "If someone planted a bomb down there I may never speak to you again, Dick. You should have searched further!"

Captain Gringo said, "I looked around as much as anyone could without hauling half the cargo up on deck. Nobody aboard would be crazy enough to sink the schooner under them. By the way, speaking of crazy, that Greek boy, Socrates, sure gets around. They say he's been screwing that Swiss, Fitzke, now.''

"Sacrebleu, I am beginning to feel so left out. I thought you said *Keller* liked boys.''

"That's what his wife told me, before she changed her story. Maybe Keller and Socrates had a lover's quarrel and the Swiss caught him on the rebound?''

Gaston laughed and said, "I wish that Hungarian, Horgany, would go to bed with Socrates so I could get a crack at that little Eva! Alas, they seem a devoted couple, even though she does have the eyes of a dedicated sex maniac.''

Captain Gringo told him to stop talking dirty and let him get some sleep for chrissake. It was bad enough a guy had to turn in earlier than planned with an only partly satisfied erection. Now the noisy old bastard had to remind him of stuff he hadn't even been thinking about.

He turned over and tried to fall asleep. He wondered if Antigone, or Herta, was hurting for him right now. He wondered what that little Oriental-eyed Eva looked like with her clothes off, and if Horgany was treating her right right now. Jesus, he was never going to fall asleep at this rate, tired as he was. But then he did, and didn't stop to dream until just before Gaston woke him up, saying something dumb about something on deck.

Captain Gringo sat up, rubbing his face, and muttered, "God damn you, Gaston. I was having this dream and somebody was telling me something important, if only I could remember who it was or what they were telling me. What time is it?''

"About seven in the morning, and wait until you see

what's come up with the sun! It looks like a Carib canoe, adrift, and the lookout does not think it's empty. He just called down that there is a naked lady lying down in it off our bows!''

The lookout wasn't drunk or crazy. As Captain Gringo and Gaston joined the crewmen in the bows, the *Peirene* lay dead in the water, gently riding the long glassy ground swell as the second mate and bos'n gently hauled a stark-naked girl aboard from her semiswamped dugout canoe She was unconscious. That was the only reason she wasn't putting up one hell of a fight. For the more worldly soldiers of fortune could see at a glance she was a Black Carib, no more than fourteen or so, with her firm young body too dark for pure Indian but too red for pure black or mulatto.

Venezis still thought he'd rescued something less inclined to kill on sight, of course, so as they approached he turned and said, "There is no paddle aboard the canoe or adrift in sight. She must have lost it and been swept out of the mouth of some river over that way, no?"

Captain Gringo said, "No, she's not a Mosquito. The first thing we do is tie her hands and feet. Then we'd better take her canoe in tow and wake her up with some brandy. I doubt it, but she may speak a little Spanish."

Venezis frowned and said, "We'll make her comfortable in my quarters and give her some ouzo. But it seems silly to tie her up."

Then the naked girl opened her eyes, murmuring in quite human discomfort until she looked up at the Greek seamen holding her and showed Ilias Venezis what a Black Carib behaved like, thinking she'd been captured by the white men she'd been raised to hate.

The Greek who'd been gently supporting her howled and reared back, clapping a hand to his face as four claw marks spattered blood across the deck. The second mate tried to grab her from behind but made the mistake of uttering soothing remarks to what he still took for a little girl, until she put him on the deck with a kick in the crotch. So when she screamed like a banshee and staggered aft along the deck, it was all hers, even if she didn't know where she was going.

Venezis gasped. "My God, what's *wrong* with her?"

Captain Gringo said, "Spanish slavers, for openers. I'll get her when she falls again. She's too weak and groggy to really sink the ship with her teeth right now."

He saw he was right when the Black Carib girl staggered into the fore-cabin coaming, tried to tear the roof off, and fell unconscious to the deck again as Gaston whipped off his belt and said, "I'll get her wrists. Someone get those ankles before she wakes up again, dammit!"

Captain Gringo dropped to his knees to hold the girl's ankles as Venezis came unstuck and produced a length of splicing cord to lash them together. Gaston said, "Give the rest to me. I'd rather have my pants falling down than a Black Carib running free on deck. But that looks better."

The skipper tossed Gaston the coil. They'd just tied her good when she woke up again, struggled madly, screamed loudly, and banged her head on the deck a couple of times to knock herself out again.

Captain Gringo said, "You don't want her in your quarters. If she can't get at you any other way she'll shit your bunk. Let's take her to the mess and put some food and water in her, for openers. She looks like she hasn't been getting either regularly, lately."

He picked her up. She was amazingly light for so much trouble. He carried her aft to the ship's mess, where by now everyone, awakened by the noise, seemed to be gravitating. As he carried the young girl through the gathering crowd he shouted, "Stand back and, better yet, get the hell out of here. This kid's scared of white faces. So it could throw her into shock to see this many gaping at her when she comes to again."

Actually, it seemed to give the Black Carib a raving fit just to see Captain Gringo, Gaston, the skipper, and Antigone Kantos when she sputtered and opened her eyes again after the Greek girl had forced some ouzo between her lips. She bit down on the tin cup with strong white teeth and tossed it over Antigone's shoulder with a jerk of her head. Then, since the startled Antigone was out of easy reach, she twisted and tried to bite Captain Gringo's face off as he held her up in a seated position atop the mess table.

He swore and flattened her gently but firmly against the table as she pounded her bound heels on the wood, struggled to free her bound hands, and cursed him and everyone else in sight in incomprehensible Carib.

Antigone asked what she was saying. Captain Gringo said, "It's Carib to me. Have you got anything back there that smells really yummy? I don't think she's getting the message that we want to feed her before we rape and torture her."

"My God, is that what she thinks you mean to do to her?"

"Can't you tell? Get some damned *food*, Antigone!"

The Greek girl dashed into the galley, grabbed the first pot she came to, and ran back out with a mess of fava beans laced with garlic and olive oil. She smiled down at the raging captive and put a spoon in the Greek cooking to let the Black Carib girl smell it.

Captain Gringo braced himself. He knew what *he'd* do if unknown savages showed something that smelled like that under *his* nose!

But apparently the pretty little Black Carib had been adrift at sea longer than they'd assumed. She went right on scowling and snarling at Antigone, but let the Greek girl feed her a spoonful at a time, the way a trapped wolf might accept its last meal.

Captain Gringo laughed and said, "I'll be damned, she seems to like Greek cooking!"

The laugh was a mistake. The young captive turned her head away from Antigone, glared thoughtfully at him, then spat a mouthful of chewed fava beans and garlic in his face.

He wearily wiped it away as he sighed and said, "Could use a little less garlic. I forgot they only allow their friends to laugh at them."

"They have friends?" marveled Venezis.

Gaston said, "Oui, but, as one might assume, not many. She probably thinks we are Spanish slavers. Please don't point out there are no Spanish slavers anymore. It's been quite some time since the last ogre ate a child in my old neighborhood, but when one is raised on horror stories, one tends to become excited when they seem to be coming true, hein?"

Having deigned to swallow a few spoonfuls of Antigone's highly seasoned beans, the young captive refused more and seemed to be asking for something. Then she remembered one wasn't supposed to ask favors of the devil and dummied up, trying not to cry. Antigone asked, "What do you suppose she's asking for?" and Captain Gringo said, "That's easy. Water. Now that we've relined her stomach and put some salt back in her, we can slake her thirst without killing her."

Antigone ran back to the galley as Venezis snorted in disgust at himself and said, "Of course. I should have thought of water right away instead of ouzo!"

But Captain Gringo said, "No. It's better to wake a dehydrated stomach up gently. I made the mistake of pouring a canteen down the throat of a prospector we found lost in the Arizona desert one time. He thanked us, threw it all up, and died of shock. I think it's the salts you lose, sweating under a hot sun. I don't know what the garlic helps, but, yeah, this one's coming back to life okay."

Antigone returned with a pitcher of water and some sweet sticky loukoumi she'd just baked. The Black Carib girl seemed to trust another female better. She may have assumed Antigone was a slave girl, too. At any rate, she let Antigone feed her loukoumi and would have swallowed the whole pitcher of water had not Captain Gringo told Antigone to take it easy. The native girl glared at him as she realized he was the head torturer who wouldn't let her have all the water she wanted.

The others asked what came next. Captain Gringo said, "We'd better lay her down somewhere and toss a blanket over her."

Antigone frowned and said, "I hardly think she needs a blanket, Dick. She's sweating like a little pig now."

He nodded and said, "Yeah, she sure was dehydrated. Now that her pores are starting to work again, she'll probably come down with pneumonia on us if we let her catch a chill. She must have been adrift quite a while to get her system so screwed up."

Venezis said, "You're right. She's starting to shiver. I once found a Turk adrift, back home, and we'd no sooner cooled him off and made him comfortable than he turned blue and died on us. But it could have been worse. At least it was only a Turk. We'll have to put her to bed. But where, if you say she's liable to mess the bunk?"

Antigone laughed and said, "Let's put her in Socrates's cubby. He's seldom in his own bunk, and what's a little skata on the sheets to *his* kind?"

Venezis laughed too, but said, "All right. But you shouldn't talk about a shipmate like that, Girl. It's not seemly, coming from a woman."

Gaston said, "I've a better idea. Why not just give her a paddle and put her back in her canoe. Look at those savage eyes glaring back at us. She shows no gratitude at all and I doubt she ever shall, hein?"

Captain Gringo said, "We're not after thank-you notes. We just have to save the poor little brute's life."

"Pour quoi? If the shoes were on the other feet the adorable child would *eat* us! Can't you see she's an untamed savage?"

"Sure, but *we're* supposed to be civilized. Let's get her into that cubby under a blanket."

They did, but it wasn't easy. The Black Carib girl wriggled like a panic-stricken snake when Captain Gringo picked her up to carry her to the mess attendant's cubby. It felt sort of sexy to him. For she was nicely built as well as naked and slippery. But from the way she was screaming she must have thought he was about to put her in the cooking pot. She seemed surprised as hell when she found herself still bound but lying on a clean sheet with a cotton-flannel blanket over her. Antigone said she'd stay with her until she calmed down, since she was the only one the frightened native girl didn't scream at.

As the men went back outside, Venezis asked how long all this would be going on. Captain Gringo said, "We're over a day's sail from the Bahías, where she must have drifted from. It looks like she lost her paddle before or after getting caught in the coastal countercurrent that swept her this far down the coast. By the time we reach her home waters, she'll have hopefully calmed down enough to tell us which Bahía she belongs on."

"How? Do you speak Carib, Captain Walker?"

"Not exactly. But we all know at least three Carib words. 'Hurricane,' 'hammock,' and 'cigar' were picked up by the early Spanish from the Indians. She may remember a little Spanish, once she stops spitting at everyone."

Venezis shrugged and said, "Well, I'm sure Socrates can find somewhere to bed down until then." The Greek skipper chuckled and added in a lewd tone, "Our Socrates has never been happier than on this voyage."

"Yeah, I heard he's been keeping his little ass busy. I wonder where, right now. I haven't seen him at all this morning. But what the hell, he's not my type."

Venezis frowned and said, "Pantocrator, you are right, and it's his *watch*, too! I'm a tolerant man, but this is too much. He's not supposed to entertain passengers when he's supposed to be on duty! Let's see, he's been bending over for that Frenchman, DuVal, so . . ."

"I protest in the name of France!" Gaston cut in, adding, "DuVal is a stuck-up species of bourgeois prick. But he is not a homosexual. He was boasting to me last night about his five children, and one must assume if a man has *one,* it could hardly have come out of a pervert's derriere, hein?''

Venezis shrugged and said, "Perhaps DuVal has been away from home too long. Perakis told Tarsouli and Tarsouli told me that Socrates spent the night in the Frenchman's stateroom.''

Captain Gringo said, "That's funny. I heard he was bending over for Fitzke, the Swiss. I forget who told me. Must have been a little birdie.''

Gaston said, "Fitzke and DuVal were both on deck when we fished that native girl from the sea. Perhaps it is someone else's turn with our Socrates?''

Venezis frowned and said, "Enough is enough. The fool is supposd to be on duty, not fucking the entire passenger list!''

The soldiers of fortune followed the skipper down the companionway, bemused. Venezis came to DuVal's door first and pounded it imperiously. The French engineer opened it, wearing his clothes and a curious look on his otherwise innocent face. The skipper demanded to know if Socrates was there. DuVal looked blank and replied, "Of course not. I have not ordered room service. As a matter of fact, now that you mention it, I have not seen the boy at all this morning. What is going on here?''

Venezis nodded curtly and marched on. Behind him, Gaston said something in French to DuVal, who gasped. "Mais non! C'est ridicule!'' and so forth until he slammed his door in a huff as the skipper banged on Fitzke's.

The Swiss looked more sleepy than perverse as he came to the door in his pajamas to ask what they wanted. Venezis stared beyond him at the empty bunk.

125

There were two bunks in the stateroom. The top one was neatly made up. Captain Gringo asked, "Doesn't Olsen share this stateroom with you, Fitzke?" and the Swiss nodded sleepily and said, "Of course. He's been up for some time, if you're looking for him. What's going on?"

Captain Gringo said, "Go back to bed. False alarm," as he hauled Venezis back and shut the door politely in Fitzke's bewildered face.

Captain Gringo said, "We'd better have a powwow with your crew. Somebody has to be fibbing like hell. They forgot Fitzke was bunking with that big ugly Swede, and I think Gaston's right about DuVal, too!"

They moved aft to the skipper's quarters and Venezis called his men in one at a time. Captain Gringo and Gaston found it sort of tedious, as neither spoke Greek. But it seemed to work out that Tarsouli had been told by Parakis, who'd been told by Savalis, that Meletzis had told him Socrates was screwing *both* the Frenchman and the Swiss.

So the skipper had Meletzis come down from the crow's nest. When confronted, young Meletzis confirmed, red faced, that he had indeed passed on the gossip. But when Venezis demanded to know who'd told *him*, Meletzis confided he'd gotten it from the horse's mouth. Socrates himself had boasted of his conquests among the passengers. Meletzis was quick to add he'd still refused the mess boy's offer to bend over for him as well.

Venezis sent him back aloft and told Captain Gringo, "There you have it. Some men boast of having had women they've never even kissed, too. Socrates seems to think he's another little Ganymede. But by the beard of Zeus, I'll show him what I think of troublemakers aboard my vessel. When *I* finish with his ass he'll be in no condition to brag about it!''

Captain Gringo asked, ''Don't you have to *find* him first?''

Venezis snorted and said, ''I'll find him, the simpering little braggart. Where could he hide aboard such a small vessel?''

It was a good question. Venezis and some of the deck watch searched high and low for Socrates, without any luck. Captain Gringo went to the Keller stateroom, not wanting to tell tales out of school. But all he found there were Keller half-asleep and Herta half-undressed and in no mood for a long conversation just now. So that was that. Socrates wasn't in any of the staterooms, on deck, or in the hold when Captain Gringo joined Venezis and Gaston down there. Antigone of course had taken the bedding from the empty crate back to her own quarters long before this time, but Gaston, damn him, was sniffing around and called out from the corner, ''A-hah! Someone has been using this empty packing case as a love nest! My ancient and adorable nose never misses the scent of . . .'' and then he caught Captain Gringo's eye and finished lamely, ''asshole.''

Venezis didn't seem to care where Socrates may have been making love aboard the *Peirene*. He took the more logical view that it was more important that his swishy mess boy had obviously gone *over the side* sometime in the night!

He said, ''This is too much! First Papadakis and now Socrates! Do you think we have a murderer on board?''

Captain Gringo shrugged and said, ''Well, they were both a little strange, and you do have low rails for sure.''

''Dammit, they were both seamen, whatever other

odd habits they may have had. Wait! Remember how we searched for the source of mysterious noises in this very hold not long ago?''

Captain Gringo remembered the skipper dismissing those footsteps as shifting cargo, too. But he nodded and said, ''Yeah, it could have been Socrates and some, ah, friend down here. We never thought to look in that empty case. But I don't see how he could have gone over the side from down *here*. Do you?''

Venezis said, ''No. But what if he managed to seduce someone on board who later had second thoughts? We are all men of the world. You surely know how an idea that seemed quite reasonable with a raging erection may strike one as disgusting in the cold gray light of satisfaction, eh?''

Gaston said, ''You would make a good policeman, Venezis. I confess I have often wanted to throw someone I woke up with on a Monday morning overboard. I might have really done so, had I ever come to my senses in the arms of an ugly *man*!''

Venezis nodded and said, ''That must be the answer. Someone who's been at sea too long gave in to the sodomite's persistent flirting, realized he, too, had left himself open to the contempt of real men, and decided to get rid of the evidence by simply pushing Socrates over the side. But it could have been anyone and . . . Wait. We can easily eliminate the *women* on board, eh?''

Captain Gringo nodded, but he wasn't all that sure. Herta Keller, for one, had had a pretty good motive, and she was one big dame. Aside from that, the killer could have had a less-obvious motive. A pansy who got around with his trays as well as his twitchy tail could have *found out* something he wasn't supposed to know, and that worked even better.

They didn't find out how Socrates had gone over the side. But since nobody else did in the next twenty-four hours, everyone aboard but the Black Carib girl calmed down, and even she had stopped raging and struggling with her bonds by the time the lookout spotted the palms of the Bahías on the horizon.

They brought the now fully restored native girl on deck, and she just growled like a caged animal when Captain Gringo pointed and tried to get her to tell them which way she wanted to go now. He said, "Well, we're out beyond the countercurrents and she has to live *some* damned where around here. We'll just put her back in her canoe with an oar and some provisions and let *her* figure it out."

Venezis put *two* spare oars as well as enough food and water to last her a couple of days in her canoe as Captain Gringo untied her, ducked the beautiful right cross she threw at him, and let her figure out that she was supposed to drop over the taffrail into her dugout. She did, with a very bewildered look, and was trying to paddle away even before the crew untied the painter and cast loose. She paddled like hell until she was out of pistol range, then turned and shook her fist at them.

Captain Gringo laughed and waved bye-bye. This seemed to confuse her even more. But she grimly began to paddle away as if she knew where she was going.

The Jamaican, Forsythe, who'd been watching from a safe range at the rear of the crowd, laughed and said,

129

"That fool girl's going to get lost again. *Ain't* no islands off the way she's headed."

Captain Gringo stared beyond the determined girl and her canoe and, sure enough, saw that she seemed to be headed for empty horizon to the northwest. He said, "She's making a beeline and she knows these waters better than any of us, Jamaica. How do you know there's nothing over there the way she's headed?"

"If they is, they ain't on no *map*, Mon."

"Hm, I don't think Black Caribs read the same navigation charts as we do. Let's give her a good head start, then sort of tag along."

Forsythe protested, "The main Bahías is dead ahead, Mon!"

But Keller, who'd been listening, said, "Walker has a good point, you know. If that wreck lay along a *mapped* coast, the others searching for it should have found it by now."

"How you know they hasn't, Mon?" asked Forsythe. Then he grinned sheepishly and said, "Yeah, right, they wouldn't be trying to *stop* us if the game was *over*!"

Venezis didn't care if they found the wreck or not. So he didn't argue when Captain Gringo told them to let the girl get them hull down behind her and follow dead slow with the lookout keeping her in sight.

The next few hours went dull as hell. Moving no faster than a paddled canoe, the sponge schooner wallowed like a dead whale and sweated like a pig under the hot tropic sun. Tar bubbled from between the deck planks and the sponges rotting in her rigging didn't smell so great either. When someone was dumb enough to bitch about the trades being light today, Captain Gringo pointed out that they couldn't have put the native girl over the side in fresh winds.

As it was, she should have been pooped by now. But as the lookout kept her just in sight she just kept paddling as if her life depended on it, and by late afternoon the lookout called down that there *was* land ahead after all.

Captain Gringo turned to the skipper and said, "Let's heave to and let her make her home shore on her own."

"Don't you want to see where she lands on that unmapped island?"

"Why? We're looking for a sunken submarine, not *her*. She may rate a welcoming committee and we don't want to spook them by making it obvious we've followed her. The island is what we were looking for, and, if it's inhabited by people half as wild as she was, I sure hope we can spot that wreck without having to make a landing!"

It was a pretty good plan. But then the lookout called down another vessel astern and added it was hull down and seemed to be staying there with *its* lookout looking at *him*, like a big-ass bird.

Venezis said, "Skata! Someone's been following us as we followed that native canoe, the stupid sons of the bitch!"

Captain Gringo said, "Oh, I dunno. They're at least as smart as we were. But let's make 'em work at it. Now that we know where the island is, we'd better hoist sails and motor due east toward the main Bahías."

"Why hoist canvas? Even if the trades were fresh we'd be sailing against them in that direction!"

"I want us nice and visible. If their lookout's just poking his head over the southern horizon at ours, he

131

can't see the island from there. Do you really *want* him to see the island, Skipper?''

Venezis swore and started yelling in Greek as he caught on. So the *Peirene* was soon moving full speed to the east with the distant mystery ship ghosting east with them, just over the horizon. Captain Gringo said, ''Don't race them until the sun goes down. If we lose them they could circle to find us and stumble over that island they don't have on their charts, see?''

Venezis growled, ''I don't think I *can* outrun the bastards. They don't seem to be having any trouble keeping abeam with us. They must have a serious engine, too, eh?''

''Yeah. Hakim must not be the first guy who's ever thought to disguise a speed boat as a tramp schooner. But what the hell, it'll soon be getting dark and the moon's not due to rise tonight until almost an hour after sunset.''

They plowed on and at least it was cool on deck now, thanks to their headway against such wind as there was. So everyone wound up on deck. Herta Keller looked as if she was trying to tell Captain Gringo something with her eyes as she passed them, circling the deck without her husband. But he didn't follow. The sun behind his back was getting lower by the minute and this was no time to flirt with dames.

It got even more important to remain near the helm and rear machine gun when the lookout shouted down in Greek and the skipper said, moaning, ''Oh, no, there's a smoke plume dead ahead! There's either a steamship or a gunboat dead ahead! What do we do now?''

Captain Gringo looked back over his shoulder and

said, "Steady as she goes. It'll be dark well before we meet whatever it is to our east."

"Shouldn't I at least slow down?"

"No. Let everyone *guess* we're afraid of meeting patrol craft. We're supposed to be an innocent sponger, dammit!"

"That other schooner off to the south knows we're not."

"So what? You want a *patrol boat* chasing us all night, too?"

For an erstwhile sponge fisherman, Venezis was a pretty quick student. He told his helmsman not to veer suspiciously as the lookout called down that he could see where the smoke was coming from now, and that it was for sure a patrol craft, albeit a battle cruiser, not a gunboat.

Aboard the souped-up schooner ghosting them, Oburst Jager was getting the same dismal news from his own lookout. He swore and muttered to his own skipper, "Zum Teufel! Why on earth would they be headed to meet that British cruiser? Can't they see where they're going?"

The German naval officer disguised as a merchant skipper said, "That Basil Hakim has connections at the British court, nicht wahr?"

Jager said, "Ja, but unless that treacherous Greystoke knows of our telephone tap . . . Ach, that's it! The whole thing is another sneaky British trick! Damn them, they never play fair! Even when Der Kaiser was a little boy and went to visit his grandmother, Victoria, at Windsor Castle, he says the British children got nicer presents at Christmastime."

The skipper had never met Der Kaiser. So he just asked, "Steady as she goes, Herr Oburst?"

Jager hesitated, then said, "Nein. I am not ready to tangle with a British cruiser until Der Tag arrives. We'd better sheer off for now and hopefully pick up Hakim's schooner again in less-imposing company."

And so a few minutes later, aboard HMS *Malta*, a bridge officer knocked politely but persistently on the door of his captain's quarters until the old man woke and sputtered, "What? What? Come in, God damn your eyes!"

The bridge officer came in to find the captain propped up in his bunk, bleary-eyed. He wasn't sick or drunk. He'd manned his bridge all the way from Kingston on some sort of fool's errand for British intelligence and he was as worn out as his antique boilers. The younger officer who'd relieved him on the bridge said, "Lookout's spotted two schooners against the sunset, Sir."

The captain sputtered, "What? What? Schooners you say? Of *course* there are schooners in these waters, Man! We're just off the bloody Honduran coast! You mean to say you woke me up to tell me about perishing dago sailboats?"

"Just one, Sir. One of them's moving innocently enough our way, no doubt making for the main Bahía we just passed. The other veered off to the south, about the same time our lookout spotted it. I thought you should know."

The cruiser captain rubbed his sleep-gummed eyes as he pondered the picture. Then he asked wearily, "Do we have a full head of steam yet?"

"Yessir. They fixed that trouble with the condenser about an hour ago."

"Very well. Wake me up when you overtake the one who seems so shy. Probably just a bloody smuggler.

But we were ordered to intercept some bloody schooner or other. What was that name again?''

"*Peirene*, Sir. Greek registry, working for a British subject one gathers Whitehall would like to pin something on.''

The captain answered with a snore. The bridge officer shrugged and went back up to the bridge, now that he had his orders.

And so, as the sun set with a green tropic flash, Oburst Jager found himself running for his life with a British cruiser in hot pursuit while, to their north, the *Peirene* circled sedately around to return to the unmapped island in the dark.

The moon was high and the sea was calm as a millpond as they circled the mysterious island just outside the breakers. Keller didn't like those breakers much. He explained and Venezis agreed that surf breaking against a rocky shore meant deep water farther out. It got worse when they stationed a man in the bows with a lead line. The bottom was rocky too, and twenty fathoms down at the shallowest. Venezis said, "If that Spanish vessel was driven ashore here, she went down like a rock. There's no shelf big enough to hold a big tin cigar above the drop-off in any kind of seas!''

Keller said they might be able to spot the submerged wreck anyhow, come daybreak. But Captain Gringo said, "Let's not break out the diving gear until we have a look at the lee side of the island.''

Keller said, "That makes no sense, Walker. If the Spaniards made it around to the *sheltered* side, the storm shouldn't have sunk them at all!''

"How do we know it did? What if the storm popped some rivets and salt water getting into their batteries filled the hull with poison gas? We know one guy got out, with his lungs ruined. The others might not have been as tough. But they still could have run her into a cove or, hell, a beach would be better than nothing if you wanted to get off in a hurry, right?"

The others agreed it was worth a try, since the island was only six or seven miles long. But as they cruised its dark jungle-covered coast it didn't look too friendly. There were no lights ashore, but someone among the trees was sure beating hell out of a big Carib drum. They couldn't tell if the Black Caribs were giving a party because the missing girl had made it home or if they'd spotted the schooner in the moonlight and might be feeling hungry.

They left the drumbeats behind as they rounded the west point of the island and saw lights ahead along the shore. Venezis said, "That looks like a village. I see houses. Do Caribs live in houses?"

Captain Gringo called Forsythe aft for his opinion. The Jamaican was of the opinion that Black Caribs lived in trees, and pointed out, as they got closer, that some of the buildings on shore had corrugated metal roofing. Captain Gringo nodded and said, "Yeah, electric lights, too! I'd be sort of surprised if any Caribs, red or black, had ordered any Edison bulbs lately. Looks like someone more civilized must have moved out here from the mainland. Let's put in and ask 'em why."

Forsythe warned, "They could be wreckers or worse, Mon. If that island ain't on the map, we know they ain't paying taxes to no government!"

"Hell, would you pay taxes to anybody if you didn't

136

have to? Run up to the bows and tell Gaston not to fire that forward Maxim unless he hears me popping off back there. I like to keep things friendly if I can.''

The people on shore apparently had the same idea as the *Peirene* putted in, dead slow, making for the timber wharf running out from the gravel beach. A couple of locals grabbed the lines the Greek crewmen cast them, and when the schooner snubbed its bumpers against the wharf a portly man in a white linen suit and a panama hat called out, ''Welcome, Amigos! I am called Don Diego Montez. May I ask who you are, and to what I owe the honor of this visit to my humble plantation?''

Captain Gringo muttered, ''Everyone else had better stay aboard until Gaston and I check him out. If he eats us, back off, shooting.''

Don Diego didn't seem that hungry when Captain Gringo went forward to gather Gaston on the fly and leap to the wharf. As he shook hands with the heavyset Spanish blanco, Captain Gringo explained that they were sponge fishermen, looking for sponge, of course. Don Diego smiled as if he believed them and said, ''You are welcome to fish all you like off my island, Señores. But I shall be most surprised if you encounter any sponges. My rocky domain stands with its roots in deep rough water, most of the time. The seas are quiet tonight, but even so, your divers will find the currents most treacherous and the rocks below most bare.''

''We, ah noticed the surf on the weather side, Don Diego. Tell us, has anyone *else* been diving in these waters lately?''

''Not that I have noticed, Señores. As you just discovered, this is the only harbor on my island. So anyone else interested in it would have put in here, no?''

"You'd know best, Don Diego. No offense, but I can't help noticing you keep referring to this as *your* island. How do you go about buying an island that's not on any map?"

Don Diego smiled, put a finger to a flabby cheek to pull his lower lid down in the Latin sigh for hanky-panky, and explained, "Squatter's rights. Honduras may claim the Bahías they *have* on the map, even if they don't govern them much. But I see no need to bother them with petty details, eh? They leave me alone and I leave them alone. But why are we standing here discussing it? Come up to my house, all of you. We shall try to make you welcome, and your friends aboard that, forgive me, smelly boat, would no doubt enjoy stretching their legs on land again."

Captain Gringo smiled thinly and said, "They're just fine where they are, for now, Don Diego."

The Spaniard looked hurt and made a sweeping gesture around at the handful of peones in view as he said, "I see no reason for you to act so suspicious, Señor . . . ah?"

"Walker. This is Señor Verrier. We mean no offense either, but, forgive *me*, how come *you're* so trusting? For all you know, we could be pirates, right?"

Don Diego laughed and said, "True, things are not always what they seem, although I must say your disguise is ingenious, if you are pirates instead of spongers. Let us lay your suspicions to rest at once. Come, I shall be only too happy to show you around, and, as you shall see, there is not much here to be suspicious of."

He did, and he was right, in a way. The Montez plantation was modest in size albeit a bit luxurious for the acreage he, or rather his workers, had cleared. It was hard to tell by moonlight what they were growing here. But when asked, Don Diego made no bones about its being opium, adding, "Opium is still legal in all but a few fussy countries, as you know. But since it is a luxury crop, the export duties on opium can be so unreasonable on the mainland. Let us go into the house and have some cold cerveza, no?"

They did. The main house was wired for electricity, and the beer a frightened-looking Black Carib girl in a Mother Hubbard served them was ice cold. As they sat on the veranda swigging it, Don Diego explained that he made his own ice, adding, "If you listen carefully, you will hear a dull roar in the distance. That is my internal-combustion generating plant. I'd have it even further from the house if it were not for unreasonable neighbors. But it's not too noisy to bear from here."

Gaston said it must have cost him a bundle. Captain Gringo asked about the neighbors. Don Diego said he could afford the luxuries of life, thanks to the current opium market, and dismissed his neighbors as "ignorant savages of the Black Carib variety."

Captain Gringo whistled softly and asked, "Doesn't it make you sort of nervous, squatting on the same small island with Black Caribs?"

Don Diego shrugged and said, "Not really. My guards have instructions to shoot the beasts on sight. So they stay well back in the trees with the other monkeys."

The same girl came out to refill their beer steins when the Spaniard rang for her. Captain Gringo waited until she'd left before he asked wryly, "What about her? Catch her young?"

Don Diego nodded and said, "It's impossible to tame them otherwise. I have, let's see, thirty or so domesticated natives now. All captured as children, of course. You catch them the way you catch any other apes. You shoot the mother and grab the infant before it can get away. Once they get used to sugar, salt, and, ah, discipline, they're not bad workers. Naturally, most of my peones are mestizos from the mainland.''

Gaston started to ask if he'd gotten them by shooting their mothers. But Captain Gringo kicked his ankle to shut him up, put down his empty beer stein, and said, ''It's sure been interesting talking to you, Don Diego. But we'd better get back to the schooner.''

''Not just yet, Captain Gringo,'' said Don Diego flatly.

It got very quiet for a moment. Then Captain Gringo smiled crookedly and said, ''Okay, I see you get newspapers from the mainland out here as well. But if you know who I really am, you didn't really mean I couldn't leave, did you?''

It was Gaston's turn to kick Captain Gringo's booted ankle as he muttered, ''Dick, behind you, Winchester.''

Captain Gringo said, ''Yeah, there's a bozo covering you from the shadows at the far end of the veranda, too. But I'm sure our host is a reasonable man who wants to go on living. Ain't that right, Host?''

Don Diego said, ''Don't be hasty, Señores. I am not after the modest rewards posted on your heads. I am already very rich. I *pay* well, too.''

''We're listening.''

''I have been open with you. So you know my troubles as well as I know yours, Señores. The Black Caribs we were just discussing have the odd notion this is *their* island instead of *mine*. Can you believe it?''

''Easy. Some of our Indians back in the States held similar views until just recently. But do we look like the Seventh Cav?''

140

Don Diego chuckled fondly and said, "You look like what you are, a couple of killers for hire, and I need some annoying natives killed. You will do this little favor for me, no?"

Gaston asked, "For how much?"

The Spaniard shrugged and said, "Oh, I suppose ten dollars a head, U.S., would be fair, no?"

Captain Gringo growled, "You don't put too high a value on human heads, Pal."

Don Diego sniffed and said, "We are not talking about *human* heads. Black Caribs are wild animals. My offer is not as cheap as you seem to feel it is. I estimate you'd clear at least a few thousand dollars, even at ten dollars a head, if you did a thorough job. I want them *all* wiped out, you see. The creatures breed like flies, and unless one eliminates a whole tribe . . ."

"Yeah, that's what they told us about Apache," Captain Gringo cut in, adding, "They were right. But how come you and your own gunmen need outside help if you're so brave, Don Diego?"

"Did I say I was brave? I am an opium planter, not a professional hunter, and my guards have enough to do here, keeping the workers in line. I knew as soon as I recognized you that you were just what the doctor ordered to rid us of red fleas. Please say you will do it, Captain Gringo. I would much rather be your friend than your enemy."

The two soldiers of fortune looked at each other. Neither had to say anything to know what the other was thinking. This murderous fat slob was obviously a born egomaniac who'd been smoking his own crops a lot!

Cautiously, Captain Gringo said, "Well, we'd need the machine guns we have aboard the schooner, of course."

Don Diego pouted his lower lip and said, "I don't think so. You might change your minds if I allowed you to return to your friends before you dealt with my enemies."

That was a pretty safe assumption on Don Diego's part. So Captain Gringo tried, "Look, we're good, but not *that* good! How the hell are we supposed to take a whole tribe, on their own ground, with just a couple of six-shooters?"

"Oh, I can let you have some Winchesters or, better yet, shotguns, with all the ammunition you can carry. My men have found shotguns best for close-range work in the jungle. The natives of course are only armed with machetes, poisoned arrows, and such. They usually run from gunfire. But there are just so many trees for them to hide behind out there. . . ."

Before either soldier of fortune could say what fun that sounded like, they all heard the distant sound of slapping lines, Greek curses, and a couple of gunshots. A moment later one of Don Diego's guards ran up to them, shotgun in hand, to shout. "Those bastards aboard the schooner are leaving, My Patron!"

Gaston muttered, "Eh bien, that's what I'd have done by now."

Don Diego turned to them, smiling, and said, "I'm so sorry they did not choose to wait for you, Señores. But don't worry. I'm sure there will be another vessel along by the time you wipe out the Black Caribs for us. Is it not grand that you now have no choice? It saves so much dickering."

Captain Gringo stood up, stretched, and said, "Yeah, we may as well get cracking. Come on, Gaston. Let's go play cowboys and Indians."

Gaston didn't argue. But as he rose to follow, Don Diego said, "Wait. Won't you need the shotguns?"

Captain Gringo growled, "Never mind. Right now I'm so pissed I could likely lick every cocksucker on this island bare-handed!"

Gaston waited until they were in the dark jungle, away from Don Diego and his thugs, before he asked, "Dick, why are we running around in the dark with only two little pistols?"

Captain Gringo said, "I was afraid if I stayed there another minute I'd go for the fat bastard's throat, and he does have at least a dozen hired guns to back his crazy play. We don't need guns. We need a map. I don't think Venezis would rat on us completely. He got suspicious, thank God, and got his vessel and the others safely out to sea while he still could. If he means to pick us up at all, there's only one place he'd put in. We passed what looked like a deep cove coming around the end of the island. It's far enough from the plantation as well as sheltered just to the lee of this stupid rock."

"But is it sheltered from Black Caribs, and are *we*? Listen, Dick. Is that my pitty-patting heart I hear, or something even more passionate."

"Yeah, it's a tomtom all right. But look on the bright side. If the Black Caribs are beating it over *that* way, it should be reasonably safe to head *this* way. Let's go. Pick 'em up and lay 'em down before they notice us trespassing through their woodlot."

It was a good idea, but it couldn't be done. The Black Caribs waited until the two white men had made it a couple of miles from the plantation and sat down on a fallen log to rest and get their bearings. Then they moved in, from all sides, arrows nocked, and wearing neither a stitch of clothing nor any expressions on their dark faces in the moonlight. Gaston sighed and said, "Bonsoir. Could any of you direct us to the nearest good restaurant?"

They couldn't. They just pointed and gargled until the soldiers of fortune got the idea they had two choices. They could die right here and now or go with the Black Caribs and maybe die a little later.

So they went with them. Neither commented when the natives failed to pat them down and find their shoulder-holstered guns, and, better yet, Gaston still had his dagger sheathed at the nape of his neck under his shirt.

The scouts led them not toward the distant drumbeats but to a firelit clearing ringed with thatched huts. That part looked reasonable. Then Gaston glanced up at what the Black Caribs had mounted on poles above the huts and crossed himself, muttering, "Mon Dieu!" Captain Gringo said nothing as he gazed soberly up at the human heads, lots of human heads, sun dried or smoked. The hair and bone structure gave them away as the heads of white men. At least two dozen. It was small wonder Don Diego and his thugs stayed close to home at night!

As the soldiers of fortune were marched in, people started popping out of the huts, smiling as if they'd just seen something yummy. The most impressive figure stood almost six feet in its naked, dark red hide. After that it got better. It was a dame, and not bad-looking if one admired necklaces of gleaming white bone. Her beads could have come from any critter. The thigh bone she was using as the handle of her rattle, mace, or whatever, had obviously come from a human leg.

Gaston muttered, ''All that's missing is the cooking pot. When do we make our move, Dick?''

The big Black Carib woman said, in perfect English, ''Don't be silly. Are you the ones who rescued that young girl of ours? You answer the description she gave of a tall blond leader.''

Captain Gringo smiled and said, ''I was afraid she hadn't noticed. I'm Dick Walker. This is Gaston Verrier. Can we take it the kid made it home okay, Miss . . . ?''

''She did, and I am Fisi, obeah of this island. How did you get away from that monster, Montez?''

''It's nice to know our fans have been keeping track of us. I hope you won't take this personal, Miss Fisi, but he sent us out to kill you guys. But I guess you know he's like that, huh?''

Fisi nodded grimly and said, ''We know the animal all too well. We'd very much like to have his head up there with the others. But as you saw, we can't get at him. Not with machetes and our bows and arrows. You must be tired. Come inside with me and we'll discuss what we should do with you.''

Captain Gringo didn't argue. But when Gaston started to follow, Fisi pointed at the doorway of the hut next to hers and said, ''Not you. Go in there and make yourself comfortable.'' So Gaston went. He felt a lot better about it when, inside the other hut, he found himself with two giggling young naked ladies. But he said, ''Merde alors, of all times to feel coy about removing one's shirt!''

In Fisi's hut, Captain Gringo found himself alone with the lady chief, witch doctor, or whatever. As she sat cross-legged across the little central fire from him he tried not to stare. But it wasn't easy, when a naked lady sat like that so close.

He said, "You speak very good English, Fisi."

She shrugged and said, "So do you. I had no choice. I was kidnapped by blackbirders as a child and spent some time in Jamaica before I was able to get away. I wish I spoke Spanish. I have some things to say to Diego Montez if I ever get my hands on him. But I probably won't. So what does it matter?"

He asked, in a desperately casual tone, if the heads outside had once belonged to Don Diego's hired guns. The obeah grimaced and said, "No. I wish they were. But they were just some shipwrecked sailors. My people killed them before I could find out much about them. None of them spoke English. Some begged for their lives in Spanish, of course. Don't ever ask a Black Carib for anything in *Spanish*, Dick."

"I heard. But surely there can't be many blackbirders bothering your people these days?"

"What do you call Montez, a whitebirder? He's stolen dozens of our children to grow his damned weeds. When his men spot one of us older natives they have orders to shoot on sight, and do. But we know all that. The question now is what's to be done with you and your little friend."

"What do you usually do with white guests, Fisi? Never mind, it was a stupid question, I guess."

She smiled thinly and said, "Yes, but not many white men save our children and return them to us unharmed. The girl said you didn't even rape her. What's the matter, white boy, don't you like dark meat?"

"Not that young. If *you'd* like to change *your* luck, why don't we just put out the fire, Jamaica Gal?"

She laughed and said, "You're not afraid of me. I like that. Between my size and obeah powers, most of our own men are afraid of me. But let's not be flirting with the dark stuff, White Stuff. Right now I have a constitutional crisis to solve. Under tribal law, your kind and mine are sworn enemies, see?"

"Hell, I never declared war on you, Fisi."

"That doesn't matter. We declared war on you, shortly after a crewman off the *Santa Maria* raped the first Carib girl. What you did to the *black* side of the family tree didn't make us like you any better!"

"Oh, bullshit; I'm a Connecticut Yankee, and I'll be damned if I'll do penance for any long-dead slave trader, Fisi."

"Some of them aren't so dead. But I can use that point in your favor, I guess. Tribal law also says that a friend of a Black Carib is a friend for life. So let's get back to that castaway gal you befriended. You sure you weren't even tempted to trifle with her?"

"Sure I was tempted. She was pretty, stark naked, and tied up. I guess some of the others on board were tempted too. But, hell, she was just a frightened kid. What kind of a bastard would take advantage of a tied-up teenager?"

She smiled softly and said, "Not the kind you seem to be. All right, you'll stay here tonight where none of the others less understanding can get at you. Come morning we'll take you to where your friends are waiting for you, anchored in a cove. *They'll* be safe, too, unless they're dumb enough to try to come ashore."

"Nobody's that dumb, even if they don't read drum talk. Are you sure they're there, though?"

"What did you think the drums were discussing, the

weather? You want to go right to sleep or would you rather have some food and a woman first?''

"I get a choice? I must say you folks are more hospitable than I'd been led to believe. But don't put yourself to any bother. I'm not hungry.''

"All right. I'll send you a woman.''

"What's the matter with the present company, Fisi?''

She looked startled, would have blushed had she been able, and said, "Don't joke with me, White Boy. I'm obeah as well as big and ugly. Aren't you afraid of waking up *witched*?''

"What can I tell you? You may be tall, but you sure ain't *ugly,* and if you turn me into a frog it'll serve me right.''

She laughed, proceeded to put out the fire with a big bare foot, and said, "I'll turn you into *worse* than a frog if you're just funning me!''

She decided he wasn't when he found her in the dark after shucking his duds and groping his way along the thatch to where she lay, stiffly expectant, on her sleeping mat. As he took her in his arms she sighed and asked, "Are you sure I'm not too big for you?''

Then, when she felt what he was putting into her, she moaned and said, "Oh, I think *you* may be too big for *me*! But don't you dare stop now! I told you, I'm not popular with many men and, oh, yessss! You sure do know how to make *friends,* Dick! That feels friendly as anything and, oh, faster, faster, I just *love* it!''

It was nice to meet a lady so easy to please. So he hooked an elbow under each of her naked knees, lifted her long dark legs high and wide, and started hitting bottom with every stroke, which was a new and delightful experience to her, it would seem, from the way she sobbed with joy. He couldn't tell if she was really as inexperienced as she let on. Women lied as bad as men in bed. But while her smooth moist vagina ran deep enough up into her muscular dark torso to take him as deep as he might want to go, she was as tight as that little native girl they'd saved could have been. So he was glad he'd behaved himself on the schooner, too. For this was reward for virtue indeed.

After they'd climaxed together twice, she pleaded for mercy, so he dismounted for a smoke. By the light of the match flare Fisi stared up adoringly at him and whispered, "Oh, Dick, you're so pretty."

He lit the claro and told her she was pretty, too, as he shook out the light. She snuggled closer, all six feet of her, and fished for more compliments by remarking on her size again. He said she was little enough where it mattered, and then, to change the subject, said, "You told me those Spanish-speaking guys your people killed were shipwrecked. Would that have been in the last big hurricane? I've a reason for asking."

She said, "Yes. They put in for shelter in a dumb place. The storm tides made what looked like an anchorage out of what's usually a fresh-water pond not far from here. So when the water went down they were stuck."

"I get the picture. What did their vessel look like?"

"Funny. Like that cigar you're smoking, only made out of iron. It had a little cannon mounted on a post on its deck with a bigger gun turret or something behind it. I don't know much about ships, Dick. On Jamaica they were trying to make a house nigger out of me. Till I ran off to the cockpit country where some free maroons sheltered me until I could steal a rowboat."

The idea of even a strong girl rowing all the way here from Jamaica sounded interesting as hell. But not as interesting as her description of the vessel stranded closer. He said, "Okay, they knew they couldn't get out to sea again over the bar. So they came ashore, walked into an ambush, and, hold it. They'd surely have left a skeleton crew on board."

Fisi said, "I don't know if they're skeletons yet, but they sure smell awful from shore. Nobody can go out to look, of course. Its obeah."

"What do you mean, something like taboo, Fisi?"

"I don't know what 'taboo' means. But 'obeah' means the wreck's been *witched*. So nobody can board it now. Not even you."

"Let's not get ahead of the story, Doll. Who put this curse on it, you?"

"No. Can't you feel I'm still alive, you loving man? It's obeah because some men of my tribe did go aboard, to see if those dead Spaniards had left any guns they could use against Montez. But they never came back. They just climbed into that tall part and nobody ever saw them again. Obeah *got* them, see?"

"Yeah, it would look like that from safe on shore. I don't think they were killed by a curse, Fisi. It fits with that one Spaniard throwing himself in the sea to swim for it. He must have been one of the skeleton crew and, yeah, *I'd* want to get out of a gas-filled hull in a hurry, too!"

She reached down to fondle him as she asked if he wasn't ever going to finish that fool cigar and added, "Don't worry about that obeah wreck, Lover Man. I'm not going to let you get anywhere near it now."

He laughed and said, "Hell, the gas must have cleared by now."

"What's gas?" she asked. So he made the mistake of trying to explain it. No matter how he tried, her semieducated and superstitious mind added it up the same way. Obeah was a mysterious, invisible force that could kill people. This chlorine gas the white folks knew how to make killed people. Ergo it was obeah, and she was just too fond of him to let it get him. So no matter what he said or did, and he even did it dog style before morning, Fisi flatly refused to tell him where the wrecked submarine was. It got worse. She said if anyone in her tribe told, she'd obeah *them*. So none of the other Black Caribs figured to tell him, even if he could find one to talk to!

Fisi was just as adamant in the cold gray light of dawn and, worse yet, was starting to cool off. Like him, she'd just been enjoying sex with a proper stranger, and the trouble with recreational sex was that it left everyone so damned clear-headed once it was over. When he pointed out it didn't matter if the curse killed a white man just passing through, after all, Fisi said, "Don't press your luck too far, Dick. My people understand my letting you and Gaston live because you helped that girl. They'd never understand if I lifted my own obeah. I told them anyone who boarded that wreck would die. Do you want to make a *liar* out of me?"

"No. But if we don't investigate that wreck, someone else is sure to, and they might not be as friendly."

She shrugged and said, "We'll deal with them as we deal with other unfriendly strangers, Dick. Your guides are ready to lead you to the schooner. I won't be going with you. Don't look for the wreck on your own. My men have orders to kill you if you try to lose them in the jungle."

He said, "Wait. Maybe we can still make a deal.

Wouldn't it make you a pretty good witch if you could do something about those opium planters who've been bothering you?''

"Of course. But they have so many guns.''

"What do you think we have, fly swatters? Look, if you'll show us where the Spanish submarine was trapped, we'll take out Montez and his thugs. I'll even throw in a skeleton suit and mask that ought to fit you just about right. Come on, Honey, don't be so stubborn.''

She thought, then said, ''I can't lift my own obeah before I prove I have even greater powers. First you kill everyone on the plantation. Then we'll talk about the wreck.''

"I don't want to kill everybody on the plantation. Just the ones with guns, and you agree to spare the peones and captives, right?''

"Well, we may be able to turn the captive children back into Black Caribs. All right, *they* can live.''

"The innocent workers, too, or no deal. Agreed?''

"You certainly drive a hard bargain.'' She sighed. But then she giggled and said, ''You drive lots of things hard. All right. You rid us of Montez and his guards and we won't bother the others if they leave us alone.''

"And then you show us the wreck and lift the obeah, right?''

"I'll show you the wreck. If the obeah kills you it won't be my fault.''

So they shook, kissed, and would have screwed on it if it hadn't been getting so late.

As Captain Gringo and Gaston left the village with their silent scouts a few minutes later, the Frenchman sighed and said, ''Eh bien, I don't know how you got us out of that, Dick. But forget all the bad things I've ever called you in the past. Mon Dieu, I never want to spend a night like *that* again! Where were you when I needed you? I was wedged between two prick-teasing savages and it was all I could do not to weaken!''

Captain Gringo laughed and said, ''You can't be serious! Are you saying you didn't get *any* tail last night?''

''Mais non. The très sneaky girls *tried* to trick me into exposing my hidden weapons, and my glands seemed bent on getting us all killed, too. But you'd have been proud of me, Dick. I was and am a man of steel. Do we have to walk so fast? I still have a raging erection and these pants are tight.''

Captain Gringo couldn't slow down their non-English-speaking guides. But to spare Gaston further discomfort he refrained from telling him how *he'd* spent the night.

Thanks to the size of the island and the pace set by the Black Caribs, it took less than an hour to reach the cove where the *Peirene* lay at anchor. Their guides deserted them with grunts, and when Captain Gringo hailed the schooner from the tree-covered shore Venezis sent a longboat in for them.

After a few minutes of mutual congratulations on deck, Captain Gringo called a council of war in the ship's mess to narrow the crowd down to the skipper, fellow passengers, and the adoring Antigone, who kept feeling him up on the sly every time she served another round of coffee.

Leaving out the dirty parts, Captain Gringo brought everyone up to date on the deal Montez had offered and the even better deal he'd made with the natives. Keller asked suspiciously, ''How do you know we can trust those cannibals, Walker?'' and he replied, ''They didn't eat us, exactly, and we'd have never made it back here without their help.''

Venezis frowned and asked, "You mean you didn't see the flares we sent up for you last night?"

Captain Gringo looked aghast and said, "Jesus, I hope I didn't hear you right! How the hell were we supposed to see flares through forest canopy, and doesn't anybody remember that *other schooner* tailing us? Who the hell had *that* bright idea?"

They all looked sheepish. But it was Horgany, the Hungarian, who said, "I just happened to have a flare gun along with my other emergency gear in the hold. I was only trying to be helpful."

"Helpful to whom?" snapped Captain Gringo. Then, noting the hurt look on the Hungarian's red face, he added, "Okay, you meant well. But don't ever do that again."

He started to go on to explain about the deal he'd made with the Black Caribs. But another thought struck him and he said, "Wait a second. Did anyone but you know about that flare gun in the hold, Horgany?"

The Hungarian looked puzzled. He didn't seem to get it yet as he shrugged and replied, "It's no secret what we're carrying along on this expedition. Hakim himself provided most of our supplies and salvage gear. Why?"

The Greek skipper caught on faster. He gasped. "Pantocrator! *That* must have been what someone was looking for down in the hold the other night, eh?"

Captain Gringo said, "Could be. Lucky he or she didn't get to the flares before we investigated. That other schooner would have been just over the horizon at the time!"

Horgany looked horror-stricken and said, "Oh my God, what have I done?"

Captain Gringo said, "Hopefully, nothing. We dodged that mystery ship pretty good and it's probably nowhere near right now. But just in case, we'd better get moving. Here's my plan."

Captain Gringo didn't think much of his plan, either. But it was the best he could come up with on such short notice. Gaston kept bitching that they should at least have waited until dark as the tall American led him and their picked crew through the jungle toward the plantation. But Captain Gringo told him just to pick 'em up and lay 'em down, adding, "We'll probably get killed anyway. So why waste a whole day? If we finish off Montez and his thugs by noon, we'll have all afternoon to examine that wreck, see?"

Gaston asked to be excused for the rest of the day. Aside from Gaston, Captain Gringo had taken Fitzke, Olsen, Forsythe, and DuVal along. The two married men and the other machine gun had been left aboard the schooner for obvious reasons. Captain Gringo packed his Maxim without its tripod, and the water jacket was drained. It was still heavy, even with Gaston packing the ammo belts for him.

Nobody was too cheered up about their chances when they stumbled over a couple of white corpses in the jungle, two-thirds of the way to the plantation. One lay bloody and spread-eagled on its back. The other lay face down on the soggy fallen leaves, or would have, had he still had a face. Both of their heads had been lopped off.

Captain Gringo said, "They haven't started to bloat yet. Looks like Montez sent them out looking for us. That was sure dumb."

Forsythe asked, "How come we're out here surrounded

155

by bad niggers if we're so *smart*, Mon?'' But Captain Gringo told him the white guys they were after were badder and led his combat patrol on as, somewhere in the distance, a tomtom throbbed ominously.

He led his followers within a quarter of a mile of the cleared plantation and left them with the machine gun while he and Gaston scouted the setup by daylight. The plantation wasn't set up right, according to Gaston.

As they peered out from the treeline, the Frenchman observed, ''Merde alors. The field of fire is not bad, thanks to the plantation house and outbuildings being surrounded by open fields all around. But regard how the triple-titted gunmen of Don Diego are *spread out*, Dick!''

Captain Gringo did. Don Diego was nowhere in sight. So they could assume he was in the house. Why work when one didn't have to? The morning chores were being performed by scattered ragged mestizo or native work gangs, overseen by armed guards, just as spread out. Gaston said, ''Even a machine gun has its limitations, Dick. You can no doubt drop about a quarter of them before the others have made it to cover. But after that, things get complicated, non?''

''Non. I told you we'd get them to bunch up around the main house. Run back and tell Fitzke, Olsen, and DuVal to circle around to the generating plant as planned. Then get back here with Forsythe on the double.''

Gaston slipped back into the jungle, leaving Captain Gringo with his lonely thoughts for a time. They were pissers. There were so many things that could go wrong that he tried not to think of them. But of course he did.

Gaston returned with the big Jamaican and said, ''Eh bien. Fitzke will fire one pistol shot and run like hell with the others as soon as they get away with it, if they get away with it."

Forsythe asked, "How come I couldn't go along with them, Mon? I run pretty good, too."

Captain Gringo said, "I need you and your complexion here, no offense. You'd better move along the treeline, oh, a hundred yards. Then, when I open up, you pop out and wave those innocent workers your way. I sure don't want 'em in *my* way, see?"

Forsythe nodded and said, "Yeah, I can see how a white face might make 'em nervous. Jesus, they got a paleface overseer pointing a gun at every eight or ten workers. Wouldn't it be just as cheap to *pay* the poor bitty bastards?"

"Montez is a bigger bastard, and I don't think many of them volunteered to grow his opium for him. You'd better get moving, Jamaica. That powerhouse on the far side isn't that far."

Forsythe nodded and moved off through the trees. Meanwhile, the Swiss, Fitzke, spotted the plantation generating plant ahead and told Olsen and DuVal, "I don't see anyone posted to guard it. But cover me anyway. I'm going in."

He did. The Swiss made it from the treeline to the corrugated metal powerhouse without incident. But as he opened the door a shotgun blast blew him backward, dead before he hit the ground!

DuVal swore and fired his Winchester at the dim figure of the watchman inside the doorway. He said, "I think I hit him! But it's no good now! Let's get out of here!"

But Olsen just growled and broke cover, leaping over Fitzke's body and dashing inside as, on the other side of the clearing, Captain Gringo and Gaston looked at each other thoughtfully. Gaston said, "What kind of a signal do you call that? Wasn't Fitzke supposed to fire his pistol?"

"Yeah. That was no pistol. I made it a shotgun blast and a rifle shot. Hold the thought until we see what those guards out there make of it!"

Work in the fields had stopped, but nobody was moving anywhere as they stared all around, uncertainly. Don Diego came out on his veranda, looked around himself, and then, when nothing else seemed to be happening, yelled at everyone to get back to work, before going back inside.

Captain Gringo grinned and said, "I've heard of overconfidence. But that guy must *really* think he owns this island and all the guns on it! He probably thinks the guys he sent out in the jungle just met a girl or something."

"The gunmen not wearing their heads at the moment?"

"Sure. Montez doesn't know Fisi's boys got the drop on 'em. I wonder who the hell that *was* just now. None of *our* guys were packing shotguns."

At the powerhouse, Olsen had made sure there was only one watchman on duty, and that one dead, then went to work as planned on the fuse boxes they'd hoped to find there. The Swede removed each fuse in turn and swiftly replaced it with a copper coin, short-circuiting it, as Captain Gringo had directed. Olsen knew enough about electricity to know that the slum dwellers who tried to get around replacing fuses with that trick were taking an awful chance. If Don Diego had any lights burning in his house in broad daylight, hopefully he shouldn't be too upset by a momentary flicker.

With the fuses sabotaged, Olsen moved over to the generator. The self-regulating internal-combustion engine was turning the dynamo at about quarter speed. Enough to supply the amount of power needed by such a modest plantation. The plant had been designed to supply a lot more if it was needed. Olsen wanted all the power he could get. So he disconnected the governor, gave the engine full throttle, and ran back outside as the engine roared wide open.

Olsen drew his pistol and fired it once in the air as he got back to DuVal and snapped, "Let's go. I'll race you to the schooner. It's going to get very noisy around here any minute!"

But it didn't. Not right away. Captain Gringo and Gaston heard the signal, but knew they'd have to wait a few minutes for results. They were not the only ones who heard the pistol shot, of course. So Don Diego came back out on his veranda and called out to demand who was making all the damned noise while he was trying to sleep. His scattered guards looked blank. Then one called out, "I'll go have a look, Patron! It sounded like it came from the powerhouse!"

Captain Gringo muttered, "Shit," as the guard started ambling across the field the way he wasn't supposed to be going, fortunately slowly. Then he stopped and turned as, from the veranda, Don Diego screamed, "Oh, no! My house is on fire!"

That had been the general idea. As planned, the overloaded, fuseless wires in the walls of the plantation house were spitting sparks and igniting dozens of electrical fires all through the house by now. But Montez knew only that his house was on fire and kept yelling at his men to *do* something about it, muy pronto.

They all ran for the house at once, abandoning their work gangs for the moment, and so, as they all bunched up in one place, Captain Gringo rose to his feet, braced the Maxim on his hip, and opened up on them with a deadly stream of hot lead!

It worked pretty good. As half or more fell writhing to the ground, Don Diego and the others dashed into the house for cover, which wasn't such a great idea with the house on fire and Captain Gringo raking the frame walls with slugs no tin or wooden siding was about to slow down enough to matter.

Meanwhile, Forsythe popped out of the treeline farther down and called out, "Come to Papa, Children!" as he waved the confused and frightened workers his way. They didn't all run home to Papa. But the ones who just ran were moving out of the Maxim's way, so it evened out. Captain Gringo popped the fresh belt Gaston handed him into his hot weapon and, with a clear field of fire now, proceeded to chop hell out of the plantation house while the fire helped a lot by bursting out through his many bullet holes.

Don Diego was on fire too as he ran out screaming like a stuck pig with two others following, also dressed in burning rags. The others were still waving guns. So Captain Gringo dropped them with one burst as Don Diego ran on a few yards, fell face down among his opium poppies, and rolled over and over, screaming in agony. Captain Gringo didn't shoot him. They didn't owe the fat prick any favors.

The big Yank shouldered the smoking Maxim and said, "That should do it. Let's go." So they did, calling out for Forsythe to join them. The big Jamaican's voice sounded strained as he called out from the jungle, "I can't, Mon. I don't feel so good right now."

They found him sitting against a treetrunk, holding both hands to his guts. Captain Gringo dropped the Maxim and knelt to see how bad he was hit. He was hit pretty bad. Captain Gringo asked, "Jesus, how did *that* happen, Jamaica?"

Forsythe replied, "Beats the shit out of me, Mon. One minute I was waving at everybody and the next thing I knew I was on my ass with one hell of a tummy ache! I hope you got the one who winged me, Mon."

He wasn't winged. He was dying. But Captain Gringo said, "We must have. They hardly got off any shots at all before they were on the ground roasting. Where did all the workers go, Jamaica?"

"Hell, how should I know, Mon? When they seen me go down they just kept running. That's . . . gratitude . . . for . . . Oh, shit!" And then he let go to spill blood and guts in his lap as he slumped over sideways, dead.

Gaston said softly. "He was a good man, non?"

Captain Gringo said, "Don't rub it in. It was a one-in-a-million lucky shot. We'll leave him here for now. We have to speak to a lady about a submarine she owes us."

The Spanish wreck was right where Fisi had said it was. They'd never have found it without native help. The long gray metal cigar rested on the shallow bottom of the once more land-locked lake with a good thirty feet of rocky beach between its stern and the open sea. Its decks were awash but, as Fisi had said, the conning tower and deck were high and dry. The decking was less than knee deep under the placid surface, and a dark doorway set in the side of the conning tower stood agape, as if in sinister welcome.

There was no anchorage for the schooner near enough

to matter, so Captain Gringo and the others working for Hakim had to leg it over with their gear. He wasn't sure it was such a hot idea to bring the two wives along. But when Herta and Eva heard that they meant to make camp by the wreck and work through the night if need be, they insisted on coming along. The Greek crewmen who helped them carry the gear over were smarter. They all went back to the *Peirene* and Antigone's cooking.

As Herta and Eva started putting pots and pans on the campfire by the hidden lake and Horgany, DuVal, and Olsen pitched the tents and piled the gear neater, Captain Gringo, Gaston, and Keller paddled out to the wreck in a dugout provided by their spooky Black Carib friends. They had to paddle their own canoe because once the natives had shown them the place they'd all run off to avoid its obeah. Even after they'd given her a swell spooky skeleton suit Fisi insisted the wreck was cursed and that they were on their own.

As the dugout bumped against the submerged steel hull and Gaston leaped aboard in ship-deep water to secure it, Keller sniffed and said, "My God, what's that awful smell?"

Captain Gringo said, "Obeah. I sure hope you guys can tell what went wrong without having to go below. Don't bodies pickled in salt water smell swell?"

As they all got aboard, sort of splashy, Keller waded about a bit and said, "The hull seems sound enough, topside. I don't see how they could have taken green water aboard, even in a bad storm, even with that one hatch open."

"I was afraid you'd say we have to look at the bottom. I wonder if we can get at it from inside. Unless that was an awfully big minnow I just saw over that way, the storm trapped some sharks in here as well. I doubt they've been getting much to eat in here, cut off from the sea so long.'' He waded to the open hatch, looked in, and added, ''Oh boy!''

The inside of the conning tower was of course flooded shin deep. But that wasn't what bothered him. The two bare bloated corpses floating face down in the fetid water looked too rotten to move without having them fall apart and stink even worse.

Keller gagged at the reek of rotting flesh but was man enough to sniff and say, ''I don't smell any chlorine now.'' So Captain Gringo said, ''By now the batteries have been washed clean. Unfortunately for these two Black Caribs, they came aboard too soon. The rest of the crew must be below, unless some got over the side to feed the sharks a light snack. It looks like you're going to need your diving gear, Keller. Unless you can tell something from the few pipes and gauges I see in here.''

Keller muttered something about his hard hat and pump as he stepped inside gingerly, avoiding the dead natives, for an examination of the little visible evidence. Captain Gringo and Gaston remained outside. They didn't know beans about submarines and the smell was bad enough on the shin-deep deck.

Keller soon came out, gasping for air, and said, ''Nothing. Nobody opened any wrong valves. Not that I'd have expected them to. They were running on their internal-combustion engines when they went aground in here. That's no surprise, either. They'd never have found this inlet had they been running submerged on their batteries on a dark stormy night.''

''The batteries were fucked up with sea water anyway, right?''

"We don't know that. The sea water may not have gotten to them before they grounded. If you want an educated guess, I'd say it appears they ran for what they thought was shelter, grounded on a rocky bottom, and sprang a leak. Probably not such a bad one, if there was time for *anyone* to get out, with the flooded batteries generating poison gas inside."

Gaston looked down at his submerged feet and said, "Merde alors, I'd never call what happened a slow leak!"

Keller shrugged and said, "It's been here long enough to fill with water from a bathtub tap. I'll know more once I have a look below with my diving gear. But I don't think we have much of a mystery here. The Spanish crew displayed just plain poor seamanship. They'd have been all right if they'd just ridden out the storm in a watertight vessel. But they chose to run it aground on rocks, like greenhorns."

Captain Gringo said, "We'll have to do better than that if we expect Hakim to pay us off. The Spanish navy may or may not have been dumb enough not to pick a crack crew after spending so much money for this cigar. But I'm betting her skipper had his *reasons* for putting in here and I imagine Hakim wants to know why, too."

So they went ashore to break out Keller's diving outfit. But it just didn't seem to be Keller's day. He swore in rage as he hefted his hard hat and said, "The goddamned glass plates are missing! Who in the hell could have stolen them, and why?"

As the others gathered around, concerned, Captain Gringo took the helmet from Keller to examine and growled, "The *who* was our mystery guest in the hold the other night. The *why* is easier. Nobody would notice clear glass missing, down there in the dim light. The glass wasn't broken out. I can see the bastard simply unscrewed them quietly. I'd say someone doesn't want us looking too closely at that wreck's pressure hull, unless we have a mad glass collector among us.''

The others started looking at one another uncertainly. Then Herta Keller asked, ''Couldn't it have been that Greek, Socrates? *He's* missing, too, nicht wahr?''

''That might work,'' Captain Gringo said dubiously.

Keller said, ''We don't know he drowned. There was that other schooner skulking somewhere near us, and if he just dove overboard with a life jacket or a float . . .''

''He could have been that brave, or dumb about sharks,'' said Captain Gringo, ''but we're not going to be able to ask him about it now. How long would it take to cut new helmet ports if Venezis can spare us some glass, Keller?''

''Are you crazy? That wasn't *window glass* the son of a bitch stole from my helmet, dammit! It would be suicide to dive without the original tempered, shatter-proof ports!''

Horgany suggested, ''The water out there isn't very deep. Perhaps if we tried simply swimming down with our eyes open underwater, eh?''

Keller told him he was crazy, too, and Captain Gringo had to agree to the extent of mentioning the shark or more he'd spotted circling the wreck. Then he said, ''Of course, if a guy who enjoyed holding his breath a lot were to swim down *inside* the hull, with a waterproof flashlight . . .''

Keller said, ''Be my guest. Aside from God knows what sort of wreckage clogging the passages down there, the other dead bodies should be lots of fun to swim through!''

Captain Gringo shook his head and said, "I'd be no good down there. I wouldn't know what to *look* for, even if I managed not to drown. Hakim wants a report on the tub's naval architecture, not heroics."

Olsen said he was willing to try. Captain Gringo didn't ask the big Swede if he could swim. He asked if he was a naval architect. When Olsen said he just knew guns and engines, the American told him to forget it, explaining, "We know their engines were running, until they ran out of ocean. The question is why they made for the nearest uncharted shallows when they could have simply submerged and ridden the storm out below the wave surge."

Keller said, "Maybe they were just chicken. It's sort of hard to get used to the idea of sinking your vessel on *purpose*, so, if the skipper was an old clipper-ship type . . ."

"I doubt that," Captain Gringo cut in, adding, "Hakim says Spain already paid good money for that vessel. No navy accepts a new ship without sea trials conducted by its own people. So Spain has to have at least a few guys who know how to dive a submarine, and it just doesn't figure they'd put a total jerk-off in command of their one and only sub!"

Before anyone could offer any further suggestions, Gaston swore and pointed out to sea, shouting, "Regardez!" So when Captain Gringo turned to look he got to swear, too. A schooner was cruising just off shore. It was not the *Peirene*.

Herta Keller screamed, "Oh mein Gott! We have to get out of here before they see us!"

But Captain Gringo said, "They might not, if we don't all yell at them at once. From out where they are, this should look like just a shallow cove, thanks to the rocky bank between the lake and sea. Let's just keep our heads and let 'em sail by. If they'd spotted us they'd be heaving to, so no sudden movements, and, yeah, they do seem to be moving on. But we'd better send a runner to warn Venezis.''

DuVal said, ''I'll go. I once won some foot races as a schoolboy. But what are your *orders,* M'sieur?''

''Tell the Greeks to get the hell out of their cove and circle back for us after dark. If those clowns out there don't spot anything too interesting, they should have given up on this island by then. Don't bother coming back, DuVal. Just get going. There's just about time if you run like hell!''

He and most of the others were staring after DuVal as the Frenchman tore into the trees, of course. So Captain Gringo's back was turned to Horgany and Eva when he heard two shots in rapid succession! He whirled and went down on one knee as he drew his .38 to see Horgany on the ground with Eva standing over him with her own whore pistol in hand, smoking. Horgany held a bigger flare pistol in his dead hand, too. Before anyone could ask why, the flare he'd fired exploded high in the sky above him, and Captain Gringo said, ''Oh, swell!''

Eva Horgany said, ''I tried to stop him. The bastard was a German spy!''

Captain Gringo lowered the muzzle of his own gun politely but kept it handy as he asked the Hungarian girl what *she* was.

Eva said, ''I was not his wife. He thought I was his mistress. He wasn't Hungarian. He was a German who spoke enough Magyar to pose as one. But Hakim is hard to convince. So he paid me to seduce this two-faced rat and keep an eye on him.''

Gaston said, "I am sure you were well paid, M'mselle. But while we are standing here discussing the past misdeeds of a dead man, that très fatigué ship out there seems to be turning about!"

Captain Gringo turned, holstered his revolver, and sighed. "When you're right you're right. Come on, let's get back out there in the canoe. I mean *now*, Gaston!"

As the soldiers of fortune ran for the dugout, Captain Gringo called back to the other men, "Get yourselves and the women back in the jungle. Far. If this doesn't work, a lot of shells should be landing around here any minute!"

As they paddled for the submarine, Gaston said, "Ah, oui, I see the plan. But how am I to fire that adorable deck gun with no shells, Dick?"

"There's a rack of seventy-fives in the conning tower. I noticed them before, but didn't think we'd ever need them *this* bad! Can't you paddle any faster, dammit?"

"Not when you insist on going the wrong way. That schooner's heaving to out there and they could have even *heavier* deck guns, non?"

"Shit, they don't even know what they're aiming for. They just stopped to figure out what that flare was all about. So we should still have surprise on our side."

They bumped against the submarine and leaped out to wade for the conning tower. Captain Gringo said, "Get on the gun and *aim* it, dammit! I'll only be a jiffy with the ammo."

He didn't take that long. As he sloshed toward Gaston and the deck gun with a heavy clip of four shells, the little Frenchman swung the German-made barrel seaward at the no-doubt German-made schooner and said, "Voilà, I can just hold them in my sights without hitting that stupid conning tower, if they don't move behind it on me!''

He opened the breech. Captain Gringo braced the shell clip between his legs and slammed the first one home, asking, "What are you waiting for?''

Gaston said, "Stand clear," and pulled the lanyard.

It didn't work as planned. The deck gun fired swell. But the steel deck it, and they, were standing on peeled up and away like the lid of a sardine can, sending the soldiers of fortune ass over teakettle over the bows and into the water!

The shock of cold brine closing over his head and ringing ears revived the stunned Captain Gringo enough to start swimming fast. It seemed to take forever. But in truth he'd made it to the shallows and was helping the groggy Gaston ashore before any shark in the neighborhood recovered from its own no-doubt ringing ears. Gaston spat brine, coughed, and asked, "What happened?''

Captain Gringo waited until they were back on dry land before he said, wheezing, "I think they should have used more rivets on that deck.''

They staggered toward the piled supplies. Nobody else was still about, of course. Captain Gringo picked up his machine gun, propped it over the piled boxes with its muzzle pointed seaward, and armed it. Gaston picked up a rivet that had flown all this way, shrugged, and said, "So much for German engineering. But why are you pointing that stupid weapon out to sea, Dick?''

"They're hoisting a parley flag out there. Have you got something white to wave?''

Gaston pulled some bedding from one of the sleeping bags they hadn't gotten to use here after all and proceeded to wave it back and forth, but said, "Oui, this should do it. But why argue when it's so simple to just run, Dick?''

"Run where? Now that those fucks know we're here, they can just lob shells at this little rock until it sinks. Heads up. They've seen our bed sheet. They're putting a boat over the side.''

The soldiers of fortune waited until the landing party from the mystery ship grounded on the barrier beach. Then as the eight men from the longboat stood marveling at the hidden lake and wreck between them and the forted-up soldiers of fortune, Captain Gringo fired a short burst of automatic fire to show them he wasn't a sissy before he called out loudly, "Over here. We'll talk to just *one* of you!"

The distant figures went into a huddle. Then one started walking around the lake alone, hands polite. Captain Gringo waited until he'd made it around to their side and gotten within speaking distance before he snapped, "Far enough. State your name and business, Pal.''

The man, dressed in ordinary seaman's clothes but standing as if he had a ramrod up his ass, clicked his heels and said, "I am an officer and a gentleman. I am not at liberty to tell you more.''

"That's okay. I know a German accent when I hear one, Fritz. I used to be an officer and gentleman myself. Do you want to make a deal?''

"What kind of deal, Mein Herr? As you see, resistance is useless. But all will go well with you, if you obey.''

"Bullshit. We can still make you fight for the prize, and even if you win, it's going to cost you.''

"Be reasonable, Captain Gringo. You can't even hit my schooner from there with that machine gun. But I

170

assure you our new Krupp deck guns can hit anyone on this island!''

Captain Gringo lit a smoke as he let Jager stare into his machine-gun muzzle awhile before he said, "I'm willing to be reasonable if you are. You see the wrecked Spanish sub we've all been looking for. It's no use to us. But you can have it if you agree to my terms.''

Jager turned on one heel to stare soberly at the now-more-wrecked-than-ever wreck for a time before he turned back and demanded, "What are your terms, Captain Gringo?''

"If you know who I am, you know I can make life rough on any salvage crew you try to send ashore. But, like I said, the wreck's all yours, provided you agree to the following. One: your people land here and nowhere else on the island. Two: you salvage, examine, eat, or whatever that wreck and nothing else. Then you get the hell out of here.''

"What is your number three?''

"There isn't any number three. I'm offering you the wreck free and clear and you're agreeing not to bother anyone or anything else on the island. I may be doing us both a favor. The natives are sort of restless and I have a terrible temper when I'm double-crossed, too.''

Jager smiled thinly and said, "So I have been told. Hakim's people have of course already examined the wreck, nicht wahr?''

"Not really. The German agent you put aboard fucked up our salvage gear. You don't have to worry about picking him up before you leave, either. Horgany's body is over here behind these boxes with us. You can bury him or stuff him or whatever without even entering the treeline before you go. How do you like it so far?''

Jager chuckled and said, "You seem to have thought

171

of everything. How did you find out about our man on board?''

''That was Horgany who fired the flare for you just now. Need I say more? If you want to bicker about details we can give you a pretty good fight. If you're smart, you'll see it's just not worth it. So let's hear your terms.''

Jager saluted stiffly and said, ''I agree to yours. But no tricks, ja? I agree not to fight if you give me no cause to fight you. I do not mean I am *afraid* to fight you if you are planning *treachery,* Captain Gringo!''

''What can I tell you? We both went to military school and we both know the rules. Go back to your landing party now, and give us ten minutes to clear out.''

''Don't you trust me, Captain Gringo?''

''About as well as you trust me, Square Head!''

Jager laughed and turned away to rejoin his men. Captain Gringo waited until he was out of range and told Gaston, ''Okay, let's get out of here poco tiempo.''

Gaston grinned slyly and said, ''For once we agree on something. But just how are we to cross those Boches double without getting our adorable derrieres shot off now?''

Captain Gringo said, ''We can't. Not without big guns of our own. We'll find the others, move everyone over to what's left of the Montez plantation, and build a bonfire for Venezis after dark. He'll spot it from sea and put into that wharf to pick us up, I hope.''

''What if those Boches spot it as well?''

''They won't, if they're here trying to figure out what went wrong aboard that sub they sold Spain. If they plan a double cross, we should know it before nightfall. Some are sure to get off at least a few shots before the Black Caribs whack their heads off in the jungle.''

As they walked through the same jungle, Gaston thought a bit and said, "Eh bien. Even a Boche should be able to see the disadvantages of treachery after you've made it so easy for them to get what they want. Why did you make it so easy for them, Dick? It's not like you to give up without a fight."

"Shit, trying to stop them now wouldn't be a fight. It'd be plain suicide."

"True, but I have seen you standing up to greater odds, you noisy child. I imagine Hakim was expecting a little more for his money, too."

"Fuck Hakim. He didn't offer us enough to get us all killed for him, you know. Come to think of it, *nobody* has *that* kind of money!"

"I agree. But unless Hakim does, he's not going to pay us at all."

"What do you want, egg in your cerveza? You're the one who's always bellyaching about taking chances. I should think you'd be happy for a change, to get out of the mess without further risk to your ass."

Gaston frowned and said, "I would, if we were not giving in to a Prussian species of motherfucker, Dick. But there is something about a Boche that brings out the Frenchman in me. I still owe them for the time they fired on a French truce flag in seventy. So if you have any second thoughts, I am with you. God owes me at least one more German in my sights before I call it quits!"

But Captain Gringo didn't double-cross the Germans, and, as Jager kept his end of their armistice as well, things started to go right for a change. The soldiers of fortune found the other survivors in the jungle and led them to the Montez plantation, where they found a few liberated workers had returned to their few unburned shacks and didn't seem to want anything to do with the obviously crazy gringos.

That night they built a bonfire on the beach and around ten o'clock the *Peirene* came in cautiously to pick them up. Venezis asked where to, next, and seemed delighted when Captain Gringo told him to make for Limón muy pronto, just in case the Germans had second thoughts about the deal.

Apparently they didn't. For by dawn they were well under way southeast, with not another sail in sight.

By this time Captain Gringo was feeling a little bushed. So he went below to turn in, alone. They now had a lot more room to spare than they'd started the voyage with. So he was flaked out in one of the spare staterooms, naked and trying to sleep, when he heard a discreet tap on the door and, thinking it was Antigone, got up to let her in without bothering to pull his pants on.

Eva Horgany, or whatever her name was, gasped in dismay as she saw his nude flesh and welcoming semierection. But she slid in fast and locked the door behind her, saying, "Dick, we have to talk. You got us off that island alive, but you may have gotten us all killed anyway!"

"We who are about to die salute you. If you don't intend to take off that dress I'd better find a towel or something. I wasn't pointing a weapon at you personally, Eva. I thought you were someone else."

She batted her Oriental eyes knowingly and said, "I know about you and that German slut, Herta. I hope you found her amusing as she spied on you."

He moved over to the bunk and sat down, draping a pillow across his lap as he frowned up at Eva and asked, "She's a spy too? Who sent her to spy on me, Der Kaiser or Hakim?"

Eva sat beside him and said, "Neither. That fake Hungarian was the German spy and I'm Hakim's ears and eyes on board this vessel. Herta and her husband are working for Linke-Stettin. They never really fired him at their Kiel yards. It was all a ruse."

He frowned and said, "Keller was planted by the firm that built that submarine for Spain? Hell, if anyone had the blueprints it should have been them. But, yeah, I noticed how reluctant he was to dive. Okay, so Keller stole his own helmet glass so he wouldn't have to. Is he really bisexual as well?"

"Of course. They both are. That's what makes them such a great team. What did Herta get out of you? I know *I* didn't tell her anything when she made a lesbian pass at me one night."

He chuckled and said, "She didn't get any *information* out of me, at least. I didn't have any to give her. You sure must listen at keyholes a lot, Eva. Who else was that big blonde getting, ah, information out of?"

Eva grimaced and said, "Anyone she could get alone for a few minutes, I imagine. I only know for a fact she seduced Fitzke and, of course, your friend Gaston."

He laughed and said, "Always knew Gaston was a sneak. Yeah, that was why she cooled off so sudden, once she saw she wasn't getting anything but slap and tickle out of anyone. I've got to hand it to her, though. She told a pretty good story about her husband and her not getting along, and, hold it, she must have been the one who spread stories about that poor Swiss being a sissy too, right?"

Eva shook her head and said, "No, Socrates just liked to boast. That's why Keller shoved him overboard. He enjoyed a change of pace as well as any other sodomist, but he didn't like his lovers boasting of it. Killing Socrates also clouded the sabotaged helmet, no?"

He grimaced and said, "You sure paint a pretty picture of that pair. What do you think Hakim will do to them, once you tell him all this?"

She said, "That's what we have to talk about. I don't think I want to face Sir Basil now that we've *failed* him. I have a little money. But I don't know my way around in Costa Rica as well as you do. What would it take to convince you that you should let me hide out with you until Hakim gets tired of looking for us and goes somewhere else to cause trouble?"

He frowned thoughtfully and said, "I don't see how I can do that, Eva. You see . . ."

But she didn't let him explain further. He'd noticed she could move fast when she thought she had to. But it was still a surprise, albeit not an unhappy one, when she wrapped her arms around him and with no further ado proceeded to French kiss him and jerk him off at the same time.

He came up for air, protesting, "Hey, don't waste me in mid-air, for God's sake. I've got a better place in mind to come, if we're going to be such good friends!"

She laughed lewdly and shoved him flat on his back to hook a petite thigh across him and impale herself on his raging erection. He hadn't *thought* she was wearing much underwear under that thin pongee dress. She moved her internal muscles with astounding skill on his shaft as she smiled down at him and asked, "Are we really to be good friends, Darling?"

He said, "Oh, yeah!" as he started to undress her while she slid up and down, gripping tightly, and added, "Let's see what else you have to offer."

She said, "Everything I have is yours, Beloved. Do you like my pussy? It is yours." And when he peeled her dress off over her head she held her perky little breasts up for inspection and said they were all his, too. So he rolled her over on her back and kissed them both as he pounded her and climaxed in her almost at once. She felt it and sighed. "You will save my life, won't you, Darling?"

He said, "Can't talk right now. Too busy," as he kept on moving in her delightful interior.

She sobbed, "Oh, yes, bus me, bus me, bus me!"

He didn't ask her what "bus" might mean in Hungarian. There were some things a guy could figure out all by himself. It sure was a funny word for "fucking." He wondered how a Hungarian caught a regular crosstown bus.

Eva didn't see fit to tell him the Hungarian for "coming." She just let him know by trying to bite him off at the roots with her amazing little snatch as they both went crazy for a while. Gaston had been right about her being a wild-thighed as well as wild-eyed little thing. Some of the positions they wound up in were obviously impossible. But she was pretty as well as double-jointed, so what the hell.

After having bused him crosstown, uptown, downtown, and straight up and down, Eva stayed plastered against him, begging for her life, as he lit a claro to figure out what day it was at least. She kept saying the Merchant of Death would surely kill them all for failing, until he patted her bare bottom fondly and said, "We didn't fail. I've been fibbing a lot. I'd already figured out why Keller didn't want anyone to know what was wrong with the underwater gunbucket his firm built. I knew even better when we tried to fire her deck gun and peeled the deck off. He tried to con me with disparaging remarks about Spanish seamanship. But I read my history books, and despite Francis Drake, some Spaniards know one end of a boat from the other. Hakim wanted to know how Linke-Stettin underbid him on those submarine contracts. Okay, we found out.''

''Yes, but you let the Germans recover her and now *they'll* know, too. Oh, Dick, I'm so frightened. You've never seen Sir Basil in a real rage!''

He didn't ask her if she'd ever seen the old bastard with his clothes off. He didn't want to know, and, hell, it probably would have killed a man Hakim's age. So what the hell.

He said, ''I'll handle Hakim. You can hide out with Gaston while I try to get our money out of the old shit, if you promise not to do this to Gaston. He doesn't deserve it.''

She purred like a kitten and rubbed her open crotch against his hip, saying, ''I told you, I'm all yours for as long as you want me, provided we get to *live* that long. Hakim's German rivals were not *supposed* to find out what was wrong with their design, dammit!''

He said, ''Let me worry about that. We've got some problems closer to hand to worry about.''

''Oh, would you like to bus me some more?''

''I'd like to. I'd better not. This is kind of delicate, Eva. But you see, Herta isn't the only other lady aboard I have to keep calmed down at least until we make port.''

''My God, you've been busing that Greek girl, too?''

"What can I tell you? If we're going to be pals we have to level with each other, right?"

She laughed and said, "I'll help you keep your secrets if you'll be nice to me once more before I leave, playing the innocent."

So he did, and she did, and if it took a little longer than usual with Antigone that night, Antigone didn't seem to mind.

He was just as glad he'd left Eva with Gaston, on the far side of town, when he reported to Sir Basil Hakim back in San José a few days later.

As Eva had feared, the Merchant of Death listened calmly enough until Captain Gringo got to the part about letting the Germans have the damned fool submarine. Then he said flatly, "I'm going to have you killed, you stupid son of a bitch!"

Captain Gringo said, "No, you're not. You're going to pay us the bonus and, oh, yeah, I think we rate the Kellers' share too. Now that you know they were working for your rivals. I'd like the Swiss and Jamaican's share to go to their families, of course."

"You certainly are optimistic, for a man who's about to die, Walker. I'll naturally do the right thing as far as the men who died in my service are concerned. It's good business to keep one's word. As for the Kellers, they're dead. They just don't know it yet. You can save yourself a lot of pain by telling me where Gaston and the Hungarian girl are, before your execution."

"Hadn't you better grow some before you threaten an armed adult so freely, Shorty?"

Then he noticed the gun barrels pointing out from the

drapery all around and said with a crooked smile, "Come to think of it, you do seem a little taller now. But you still don't want to have me shot."

"I don't, Dear Boy? You have perhaps one full minute to tell me why. I never sent you out to lead that perishing Jager right to my submarine, God damn your eyes!"

"I'm going to need more than a minute to explain if you don't knock off all this spooky shit. In the first place, it was not *your* submarine. It was never your submarine. Your rivals in Kiel, Linke-Stettin, built it, and you never laid eyes on it. I did. I know how they underbid you. You won't, unless you stop waving guns at people and act like a grown man, for God's sake."

"I'm listening. Keep talking."

Captain Gringo explained how Linke-Stettin had underbid him by simply building an impossibly fragile vessel that would have sunk the first time Spain tried to use it against anyone, if a storm hadn't sunk it even sooner. The old man's eyes grew thoughtful and almost amused as he heard how trying to fire the deck gun shot rivets clean ashore.

But when Captain Gringo paused for breath, Hakim wasn't smiling as he said, "All right. I know Linke-Stettin is run by shit heels. I knew that before I sent all of you to salvage their latest efforts. I'll concede you found out how they underbid Woodbine Arms, Limited. But I fail to see what good the information is to me. I already knew they hold almost anything together with haywire and spit long enough to sell it. But *I* sell weapons meant to be *used* in the field, not for show. If you'd only brought back a few more details, my engineers might have been able to design something as cheap as Linke-Stettin that wouldn't melt in the rain.

But all you did was ruin the wreck further and run away, letting the Germans have it without a fight! God damn it, man. I paid you good money to fight as much as you had to!''

Captain Gringo said, ''I wish you'd shut up and listen.''

''You tell me to shut up? You dare, with my men covering you?''

''Have to. You said I only had a minute, and I'd have been finished by now if you'd shut up and listen.''

''Keep talking. This had better be good.''

''I think it is. In the first place, there's just no way you'll *ever* underbid Linke-Stettin. If they bid any lower they couldn't even afford the haywire and spit. That's what they didn't want you or anyone else to find out. That's why they infiltrated your company with their own agents after firing Keller, they said, just for being a little fruity. By the way, you'd better not waste money having them killed. Let Linke-Stettin take care of them for you. You think *you're* mad?''

''I don't think. I am. You *let* Keller sabotage the mission, you clown!''

Captain Gringo shrugged and said, ''Couldn't be helped. Even if I hadn't been busy screwing his wife, how was I supposed to watch him every minute? He managed to keep anyone from examining the lousy underwater riveting, but it didn't matter, when Gaston and me popped all the rivets out of the top plates without really trying. So if Keller and Herta are dumb enough to go anywhere near Germany for their just deserts, I figure they'll sure as hell get them. They *really* fucked up. Linke-Stettin should be going out of business any minute, unless they want to give a lot of people their money back. By the way, was that submarine insured?''

''In time of peace? Yes. Get to the point, dammit!''

''I'm trying to. Okay, so the insurance agents will be trying to serve papers on the directors of Linke-Stettin as well. Keller and his wife may get lucky and never find them, if they have unlisted Swiss bank accounts. I know *I* sure would if I set out to cheat Der Kaiser, His Most Catholic Majesty, *and* international insurance dicks who play even rougher in peacetime.''

Hakim snorted and asked, ''Who's supposed to *tell* him all this, *me*? Unfortunately, some people just don't understand how honest I am, in my own little way. They'd never believe me if I made an obvious effort to discredit a business rival, you idiot!''

Captain Gringo reached into his shirt pocket for a claro as he grinned and said, ''I know. That's why I suckered German intelligence into doing it *for* you. Don't you suppose Der Kaiser will believe *his own* naval architects when they report to him what they found sort of melting like ice cream in the sun, back at that island?''

Hakim looked perhaps a little less like a public executioner as he said, ''I like the first part. What do you mean you suckered Jager?''

''Hell, had we simply run away and let him have it as a gift free and simple, the prick might have suspected *us* of something sneaky. Jager knew who I was. So he knew I was working for you, and you're right, people just don't understand you. They think you're a treacherous backbiting little son of a bitch.''

Hakim smiled for the first time that morning and said, ''I am. Let me light that cigar for you, Son. Are you sure you wouldn't prefer a Havana Perfecto?''

"No, thanks. Just give me the money. Got a lady waiting to spend la siesta with, see?"

Hakim reached under a silk cushion to produce a wad that would have choked a horse. But he held on to it as he said, "Let me see if I have it straight. Having outwitted the great Captain Gringo for Der Kaiser and no doubt expecting another medal for it, Jager will report he got to the wreck before you could examine *or* sabotage it. As soon as his engineers see what a shitty job Linke-Stettin did, they'll report that, too, and if you think *I* have a temper you should see *Kaiser Willy* in a snit! I *like* it. It's foolproof. Even if the directors of Linke-Stettin don't wind up against a wall, they're never going to be able to bid against me again, and I'll now be free to build all the U-boats I want to, at a modest profit of course. I pride myself on good weaponry, but I'm not in the business for my health."

"You're all heart, Sir Basil. Naturally, as soon as the Brits find out Germany's ordered a fleet of submarines *they'll* be in the market for more of the same from your *British* shipyards?"

"Naturally. It's my patriotic duty as a British subject. Let's see, here's your bonus, Gaston's, and that silly girl may as well have hers for shutting up that German spy to confuse the issue further."

"What about the shares Keller and his wife would have gotten if they hadn't jumped ship and run like hell the minute we hit Limón?"

"Don't *I* deserve anything, Dear Boy?"

"Shit, Hakim, you already *have* the money. Be a sport and I'll tell you what. I won't tell the Brits a fucking thing when Greystoke contacts us, okay?"

"Are you expecting the Brits to approach you?"

"Sure. They know you'd sent us on that mission,

too, don't they? Knowing Greystoke of old, he'll probably try to bribe me with pussy as usual. British intelligence is hard to get money out of.''

Sir Basil Hakim chuckled, peeled off the extra money, and handed it over, asking, ''Will this be enough to console you for saying no to a pretty British spy, Dear Boy?''

Captain Gringo said, as he put the money away, ''I never say no to a *pretty* British spy. But I promise I won't tell on you in bed.''

Renegade by Ramsay Thorne